BLACK SHEEP

DIRTY MAFIA DUET BOOK 1

D1479059

MEGHAN

NEW YORK TIMES BESTSELLING AUTHOR

MARCH

CONTENTS

BLACK SHEEP

Book One of the Dirty Mafia Duet

Meghan March

Visit my website at www.meghanmarch.com.

ABOUT BLACK SHEEP

From *New York Times* bestselling author Meghan March comes a story of untold truths and one man's redemption in the Dirty Mafia Duet.

Every family has a black sheep.
In the infamous Casso crime family, that black sheep is me—Cannon Freeman.
Except I'm not a free man. I've never been free. Not since the day I was born.
I owe my loyalty to my father, Dominic Casso, even if he won't publicly acknowledge me as his blood.
I've never had a reason to go against his wishes . . . until I met *her.*
Drew Carson turned my world upside down when she walked into my club looking for a job.
Now, my honor *and* my life are on the line.
Going against my father's wishes might buy me a bullet straight from his gun, but black sheep or not, it's time to make my stand.
She's worth the fallout.

Black Sheep is the first book in the Dirty Mafia Duet and should be read before *White Knight,* book two.

1

DREW

I walk into the most important job interview of my life knowing every word out of my mouth will be a lie. The résumé and references in my bag are all fake, but thanks to one of my close friends, a white-hat hacker, no one will ever know.

I will get this job. I will get my answers. There's no other acceptable alternative.

I repeat those vows to myself as I leave my security escort behind with a smile and push open the heavy carved wooden door to the Upper Ten, the most exclusive cigar club in Manhattan. Instead of smoke hanging in the air, the luxurious interior reeks of money and secrets.

Perfect. Secrets are exactly why I'm here.

"Can I help you, miss?"

A man with no neck in a tailored suit approaches me as soon as the door leading to the club foyer slips shut behind me with a whoosh of air that blows my skirt into a flutter around my legs. His bald head shines under the recessed lighting of the impressive room.

Through the thick glass wall to my left, I can see what

brings some of the richest men in the world into this insanely expensive, members-only club—a massive humidor containing row after row of wooden boxes filled with fat cigars. From my research, I know that sources estimate the value of the stock in that large humidity-controlled room at *millions of dollars.*

Hefting my bag and swinging the tresses of my long blond wig over my shoulder, I give him a sweet smile. "I'm here for an interview, actually, with Mr.—"

"She's with me." A voice, deep and smooth like the thousand-dollar-a-glass cognac they no doubt serve here, comes from behind the bull guarding the door.

My gaze darts around the doorman and catches on an imposing figure in a bespoke suit with subtle navy pinstripes. The lines hang perfectly on his tall, rangy frame.

It's him. My target . . . and hopefully my new boss.

Except the man in person is worlds apart from the man on paper. I thought I was prepared to come face-to-face with him, but mere ink on a page can't convey his powerful presence. In the high-ceilinged antechamber, his authoritative posture commands more attention than the bulk and muscle of the doorman beside him, and with nothing more than the sound of his voice.

A voice I recognize.

Not because we've ever been in the same room before, but because I went through dozens of hours of audio and video before applying for this job at the Upper Ten. I've read article after article and unearthed every available public record that hasn't been erased on this man and his family.

As I tense, I force myself to visualize him behind bars, wearing an orange jumpsuit. The exercise helps me regain my calm.

I can do this. I've done it dozens of times. Deception isn't new to me. It's my job.

As soon as I'm centered, I look up, pinning an eager, yet slightly nervous smile to my face. It's a mask, but he'll never know.

There's only one problem. When his rich hazel eyes, a mix of whiskey and bright green, collide with mine, an unwelcome bolt of heat slams into me in pure female appreciation.

No. No. No. That's not supposed to happen. Truly, this is the *opposite* of what's supposed to happen. I'm supposed to be cold and indomitable, because I knew he'd be intimidating as hell. I promised myself I'd be immune. Unaffected. It doesn't matter to me that he's the bastard son of the most infamous mob boss in the city. But my denial doesn't help, because I dismissed a seriously important fact when I was prepping for this day.

Cannon Freeman is a god among men. Shit. How is that even possible? Especially knowing what he has to be involved in?

I try to shove the annoying awareness of him aside, but it's nearly impossible while he's standing there, staring at me with those enthralling eyes.

His suit jacket clings to the sleek, strong lines of his broad shoulders and nips in to accentuate a slim waist, before his slacks hang perfectly off his hips.

Goddammit. Not fair.

Randi warned me I was underestimating him. My across-the-hall apartment neighbor told me that looking at Cannon would make my nipples peak, my thighs clench, and my brain fill with images of him bending me over the nearest flat surface or pinning me up against the closest wall. I chalked that up to Randi being . . . well, Randi. A.k.a. *Everyone's Slept with Downtown Randi Brown.* She's the kind of woman who gets men drunk so she can fuck *them*. She says her guy friends call her a dude with tits, and I can't disagree, even though she's one hundred percent female.

But the last thing I expected was for her to be absolutely right about this.

Cannon tilts his head to the side and waits for me to reply. "Unless you're not Drew Carson?" he asks with a lilt of humor underlying the question.

His rising eyebrow and questioning smirk nearly put me over the edge. *He's supposed to be a villain. A monster. How can he look like he's trying not to laugh at me in my stunned silence?*

Snapping myself out of my temporary stupor, I widen my smile and force everything aside except my goal.

Stay cool. Act cool. Be cool. That's my mantra whenever I'm undercover and things are dicey. Repeating it silently helps me pull myself together.

"I am. It's a pleasure to meet you, Mr. Freeman," I say, stepping forward to shake his hand like the professional I am.

Except there's another problem. I should have braced. I don't know why I didn't brace.

As soon as the ridges of his calluses slide across my skin and his fingers tighten on mine, another shiver of awareness shoots through me. *Why does he have calluses? He works at a desk. He's not supposed to be the definition of physical male perfection.* And yet, here we are.

"Cannon," he says, correcting me with that voice of his, which should be registered as sex in audible format. "We're informal among the staff. Patrons are another story. Treat them all like they're wearing crowns and holding scepters that can destroy your world in a heartbeat. Got it?"

While his statement is part curious and part foreboding,

his sharpened gaze takes in every inch of me, the same way I surveyed him.

"Duly noted, sir. I mean . . . Cannon." I correct myself and tug my fingers free of his, but he's watching me like he's waiting for me to spill all my secrets.

I won't, I promise myself. *Because I never have before, and there's more at stake now than ever.*

"Good. Come on. Time for your trial by fire." He lifts his chin to the bull beside him, spins around, and pushes open the next massive door.

I force myself not to grin and pump a fist in the air. *I'm in.*

My personal victory party lasts only as long as it takes to cross the threshold, and I set foot on the thick green and gold stripes of the plush carpet that so many monied, famed, and evil feet have tread.

Cannon rattles off rapid-fire orders. "I need you behind the bar. Two G&Ts, one martini—extra dirty with three olives, an old-fashioned, a Moscow mule, one Bass Ale in a chilled glass, six Perriers, and two black coffees. You have ten minutes. Don't fuck it up."

I blink several times as my brain commits the list to memory, but the question still slips from my lips. "I thought I was here to interview as a server, not a bartender?"

One eyebrow quirks as he surveys me with a tilt of his chiseled jaw. Sharp cheekbones stand out like blades in the brighter light of the club. "If you want to work here, you do what I say. If you want the job, get behind the bar. If you don't, you know where the door is. Understood?"

"Yes. Of course," I say with a chipper smile. "I understand perfectly." Silently, I add to myself, *You're a douchebag who's too attractive for his own good, and you want to see me sweat.* Not going to happen.

He doesn't know I've spent time embedded with troops

5

rushing headlong toward enemy lines. If mortar rounds exploding around me didn't shake my composure, neither will an order from the heir presumptive of the most powerful mafia family in New York. *Just the heir himself . . .* No. That was a fluke. Totally not happening again.

"I'll have those drinks for you right away, Cannon."

His hazel eyes flash brighter green with something I can't identify, but without another word, he strides away toward the long table of men inside a glass-walled room ahead of us. I'm left alone, my fingers gripping the strap of my bag as I stare after him, because *Lord Almighty, that ass should be a crime itself.*

Wait. Stop. *Why the hell am I looking at his ass?*

Randi was right. I need to check myself before I get caught up in his "superior ability to render a girl dick-struck." At least, that's how she described him. I brushed off the warnings, but they're all coming back, and fast. *Duly noted, Randi. Duly noted.*

Turning on the stacked heel of my black knee-high boots, I weave through expensive wooden four-tops and high-tops on plush handwoven carpet. I smooth my skirt over my thighs and slip behind the forty-foot-long bar that was supposedly shipped over from an establishment in Sicily that catered to only the highest-level members of a famous mafia family. Around me, the elegant brass fixtures cast a warm glow on the rich paneled walls. If I tried to imagine an enclave for the wealthiest, most famous, and exceptionally notorious men of New York City, the Upper Ten would be exactly the picture in my head.

I tuck my bag into a corner, wash my hands, and mentally prepare myself for the job to come. From inside the glass-walled room about thirty feet away from me, Cannon's head tilts back as his Adam's apple bobs with laughter. He shoots a glance over his right shoulder, and it collides with mine.

All I read in it is challenge. All I hope to convey with mine is that I'm not scared of the big bad wolf. No. He should fear me.

"Don't fuck up," he told me, and I won't.

Securing this job is all I care about right now. After glancing at my watch, I collect the necessary glassware to make the orders that will impress the man who is going to be my new boss. What a coincidence he's also the man I'm going to take down, any way I can.

You have no idea what's coming, Cannon Freeman. Not a fucking clue.

2

CANNON

*I*n exactly nine minutes and fifty-four seconds, I excuse myself from the group of senators gathered for lunch and head for the bar.

After sliding a metal toothpick through the last of three olives, Drew Carson sets the martini glass on the tray beside the Bass Ale, bubbling ever so slightly in its frosted glass.

I do a quick mental tally.

Two G&Ts, one martini—extra dirty with three olives, an old-fashioned, a Moscow mule, one Bass Ale in a chilled glass, six Perriers, and two black coffees.

My gaze lifts to her heart-shaped face and those deep brown eyes that seem like they're trying to peer inside me. Normally, when I meet someone who knows only my reputation, whether man or woman, they avoid direct eye contact. But not Drew Carson.

Whatever she's looking for, her intensity ignites a flare of fascination within me. Women rarely interest me enough for a second glance, but I have to fight to tear my attention away from Drew's blush-colored lips and focus on the drinks.

There's just something about her, and it's got nothing to

do with the way her blond locks curl perfectly over the shoulders of her feminine black suit jacket, or how much I wish I could see what's beneath those layers of makeup she wears like war paint.

When was the last time I cared about seeing a woman without makeup? Maybe never.

"I thought you weren't a bartender."

Her confident smile never falters. "I didn't say that. I just said I didn't think I was here to interview for that particular job."

And she's intelligent too. I step forward and pluck the copper mug off the tray and lift it to my lips.

"What are you—"

Before she can get her question out, I take a sip, letting the ginger flavor roll over my tongue. Sweet, tart, and perfect. Probably not much different from the woman who made it.

Whoa, Cannon. Stop that train of thought. You've known her for less than ten minutes.

Drew stays silent as I lift one glass off the tray after another, sampling everything but the coffee. I return the martini to its place with a nod.

"Come with me," I tell her, snagging both untouched mugs. "Let's talk in my office."

"What about the drinks?" she asks.

"They've already been served. I just wanted to see how you'd perform under pressure. It's time to talk about the job."

3

DREW

I follow Cannon Freeman through the Upper Ten, named for the Upper Ten Thousand, the term used to describe the ten thousand wealthiest people in New York society back in the days of John Jacob Astor and the robber barons. For this club, it's completely appropriate, although I doubt they'd even let the richest ten thousand people in the city through the door. From all my research, the exclusivity of the Upper Ten is about more than just money now.

As the luxurious carpet cushions my footsteps, two employees seem to come out of the rich wood paneling lining the walls. No, not seem. They do. Panels open like secret doors, and a man heads toward the walk-in humidor while a woman with short, dark hair winks at me as she takes her place behind the previously vacant bar.

Wait. Were the other employees in on this? Did they know their boss was going to put the new girl through his trial by fire?

I don't get the chance to wonder more because Cannon's long-legged stride stops in front of a panel, and he presses his palm flush against the wood. It opens silently.

"That's a neat trick." My comment comes out as a murmur.

Silently, I wonder what other tricks they're hiding within these walls. It reinforces my belief that I'm making the right choice. The Upper Ten is where I'll find the evidence to take down the Casso crime family and make them pay for what they did.

"Welcome to the inner sanctum," Cannon says with a wink.

No, no. He's not allowed to look sexy when I'm thinking about putting him in prison. It's clear Cannon Freeman doesn't follow the rules, and his unpredictability makes him more dangerous than I expected.

I follow him down a hallway lined with a deep green-and-gold-striped wall covering. Brass sconces decorate the walls, lending a warm glow.

After passing several closed rooms, Cannon opens a door at the end of the hallway and motions for me to precede him inside. "Once you're in, you may never leave," he says with a hint of a lazy smirk on his lips.

The comment almost throws me off-balance, but I sense that's what he's trying to do, and I keep my chipper expression in place.

"It must be a great place to work." My tone matches my expression, and his heavy-lidded stare intensifies.

Is he trying to get me to screw up?

As I step inside the purely masculine domain, I finally detect a hint of cigar smoke, mixed with the scent of leather and a tang of lemon that reminds me of furniture polish. A heavy wooden desk stretches nearly six feet across and is fronted by two green leather club chairs.

Cannon skirts around me to stand in front of the high-backed seat behind it. Floor-to-ceiling bookshelves fill the space behind him, filled with enough tomes to make it look like the office of a lawyer, not a cigar-lounge manager.

"Sit."

I smooth my skirt and lower myself onto the supple leather. As soon as I'm seated, he follows suit.

A gentleman? One would think that's the obvious conclusion, given his position, but I know better. I know what Cannon Freeman's true heritage is, and a son of Dominic Casso's could never be anything more than a savage, regardless of how impeccable his manners are or how expensive his suit is.

"I have a copy of my résumé and references if you would like them," I say, not waiting for him to break the silence hanging between us.

He settles himself into the chair and rests his elbows on the padded leather arms like a king atop his throne.

"Not necessary. I already reviewed what you submitted. You're hired, subject to a probationary period for thirty days. Full benefits after ninety. You report to Tanya, my head server. She'll show you the ropes, and if you can survive her, you'll do fine. If you can't, then my instincts were wrong. For once." He steeples his fingers as he waits for me to reply.

I stare at him like he's speaking in code and I need a key to decipher it. Nothing this important can be so simple and easy.

"You mean . . . you're hiring me? Just like that?"

"Based on your impeccable references, I knew I was hiring you before you walked in the door. You start tomorrow. Be here at ten a.m. Dress code is black and white. You're responsible for black slacks or skirt. Tanya will get you shirts in the morning before your training starts."

With that, he rises, and I get the sense that Cannon Freeman's natural state is one of near constant movement. He seems to have more energy than ten men, and it practically vibrates off him like current from a live wire.

It's as if the universe is trying to send me a warning. *Be careful how you handle this man.* I've never been great about heeding warnings, but in this case . . . I know failure will be at my peril.

I stand and hold out my hand to my new boss. "Thank you for the opportunity, Cannon. I'm thrilled to start."

My smile isn't for him, though. It's for me. If everything goes according to plan, Cannon Freeman, his father, and the whole Casso family organization will soon be in prison, exactly where they belong.

You've just let a fox into the henhouse, Mr. Freeman. Thanks for the invite.

4
DREW

Me: I got the job!

           Randi: Yasss, girl! I knew you would! Come see me. We're celebrating.

I STAND JUST outside the entrance of the building that houses the Upper Ten, debating how to respond to Randi's message. When I don't reply immediately, my phone vibrates with a text consisting of a row of emojis—two pairs of raised hands offering a double high-five, six champagne glasses clinking together, and three eggplants, which are code for *dick*.

Knowing where Randi's head is at, I'm second-guessing whether I want to meet her at Lambo's. It's a popular sports bar a block away from our apartment building, and the place I first met Downtown Randi Brown. She pulls a few shifts there a month, filling in as the owner needs her, and she's impossibly friendly.

Normally when I'm prepping to assume a new identity, I avoid making friends who can't directly help with my case. Somehow, Randi is the exception this time. She's like the puppy following you home that's so damn sweet and makes you laugh, you can't possibly say no. Except instead of being a puppy, Randi is a five-foot-ten-inch Amazon of a woman who has more genuine self-confidence than any human I've ever met. Her invitation to come celebrate is just as genuine as she is.

More emojis pop into our text chat, and I swear it's her way to sway me while she knows I'm vacillating. This isn't the first time we've played this game. I should go back to the bare apartment I've been renting for almost eight months of grieving and researching, and pore over my notes to prepare for tomorrow, but energy buzzes through my veins. I need to burn some off before I'll be able to focus.

My thumbs tap the screen before I can talk myself out of it, and not even mostly because she promised she'd tell me even more about the mysterious Cannon Freeman *after* my interview.

ME: *On my way. But skip the eggplant.*

RANDI: *Slow your roll, young padawan. Those are for me, not you. I got three on the line tonight. Can't wait to reel them all in. Get your ass over here and play wingman.*

ON A CROWDED SIDEWALK in New York City with pedestrians streaming around me like I'm an island in a rushing river, I burst out laughing with great, big body-shaking chuckles. Of course all the dicks are for her. Why would I think otherwise?

"Nice laugh you got there, sweetheart. Does a man's heart good to hear it."

A rough, gravelly voice comes from just beyond my shoulder, and I spin around and come face-to-face with a man I've never met before. But I know exactly who he is.

His steel-gray hair brushes his lined forehead, but his ruddy cheeks are shaved clean. My first thought is that his posture is too straight for a man who carries a lifetime of sins on his shoulders. He should be stooping, or at least hunching a little from the weight his conscience must bear. Except, he probably doesn't have a conscience because he's *Dominic Casso*. The head of the Casso crime family.

And he's staring at me. *Fucking hell.*

As my smile begins to fade from my lips, I jam it back into place. *Play stupid. Play stupid.*

Pretending like I have no idea who the man in front of me is, I tilt my head to the side as he holds out a tanned hand.

"I'm Dom."

I swallow hard, keeping an iron grip on my guise as I slide my fingers into his and shake his hand like I don't know he's washed blood, time and again, from that very skin that touches me.

"I'm Drew," I say, hoping the husky quality of my voice sounds like it came from my laugh and not the fact that my heart is trying to hammer straight through my chest.

"*Drew.*" Dom says my name slowly, like he's trying it on for size. Or maybe sizing me up.

I'm not exactly sure, but it's a gut-wrenching feeling to be standing in front of the man who I'm ninety-nine percent sure made the call that destroyed my entire world. It takes everything I have not to rip my hand out of his when he doesn't release it immediately.

I break his stare, because those piercing black eyes seem

to be looking for the window to my soul. Odd, considering Dominic Casso can't possibly have one of his own.

"Nice to meet you, Drew. I think we'll cross paths again. In the meantime, keep laughing, pretty girl." His assessing gaze rakes over me before he finally releases my fingers.

I break his stare and step away, wanting to put as much space between us as possible. Only then do I notice the two suit-wearing linebacker-sized men standing a pace away from us, watching the exchange with suspicion on their stony faces.

Of course he has security. I'm sure if he walked these streets without them, he'd end up dead inside four blocks.

"Nice to meet you, Dom." I get the reply out, but it's a lie, as per usual.

With a small smile, he turns toward the entrance to the building I just exited and strides away—just like his son did from me when he left me at the bar after rattling off drink orders.

I finally let out the breath I'm holding when the doors close on him and his two bodyguards. The resolve swirling in my system coalesces not into fear, but into a solid, unshakable vow.

Keep smiling, Dom. You're going to need that levity in prison.

"What took you so long, girl? I thought you flaked out on me!" Randi yells across the bar, causing every single person in the place to gape at me standing on the threshold.

For someone like me, being the center of attention is a double-edged sword. I used to soak up the limelight, but that was until I realized there were many more benefits to flying under the radar when I chose.

But as Drew Carson, the limelight won't jeopardize my investigation. My own stepmother wouldn't recognize me right now, and that's only partially because she could never be bothered with paying attention to a child who fell firmly into the category of daddy's girl. The rest of the reason? She's too self-absorbed to see through a thick layer of makeup, colored contacts, and a wig, even though she should have my bone structure burned into her brain.

Summoning my best *I got the job, it's time to celebrate* expression, I give Randi a jaunty wave. "It only took me twenty minutes."

She hip-checks a guy out of her way to get to me. "Celebration waits for no woman—or man," she says as she throws her arms around my shoulders and squeezes me against her generously endowed chest. "So proud of you. I knew you could snag that fancy-ass job."

"I'm glad one of us was that sure." I return the hug, and when we break apart, she leads me to a table under one of the dozen TVs lining the wall of Lambo's.

"Now sit your ass right here, and I'll get you some of that girly bubbly shit you like and tell my boss I'm off for the night."

"Can you do that?" I ask her, my head swiveling around to look at the packed bar and the two other waitresses rushing around like crazy people.

Randi tosses her silver-streaked black hair over her shoulder with a *pfft*. "Of course I can. I fucked him good on my break. He almost busted through the condom because he came so damn hard. BRB, GF."

She saunters away, her hips swinging from side to side like she's on a catwalk instead of a floor sticky with beer and peanut shells crunching under her thigh-high boots. Every man in the place has his eyes glued to her tits or ass, all of which are bouncing with every step she takes.

I tear my gaze away from her fishnets, booty shorts, and midriff-baring black-and-white-striped jersey, trying to guess which of the gentlemen in the bar represent the three eggplants she plans on taking home tonight. Or not even home. As Randi just proved, she's equal opportunity when it comes to hookup locations.

I don't need to be great at math to realize that would be four guys in one day if she nails the other three, after recounting what happened on break with her manager. But I'm not a judgmental prude, and what Randi does is Randi's business. She's exactly what she says—a woman who thinks like a dude and likes to hook up. To each their own.

When she leaves me alone at the table, the events of today and my encounters with Cannon Freeman and Dominic Casso rush back into my brain.

I want to say that meeting the elder Casso on the sidewalk had to be dumb luck . . . or divine intervention, but I'm not sure. Is anything that happens with the mob ever truly random? *Could they know I'm investigating them?*

I don't know how they would. I've kept my searching completely anonymous. One thing I know is how to cover my tracks, especially digitally, thanks to Ariel, my hacker friend. The pictures I've been staring at of both men for months came from my father's hidden files, and I haven't take them out of my apartment since the day I moved in.

I've devoted hundreds of hours to researching and building the case I plan to hand over to the district attorney, and after today, I've come to one very solid conclusion— those surveillance photos did neither of them justice. Dominic Casso might be turning seventy in less than a month, but physically, you would never be able to tell.

I wonder if his illegitimate son will age as well?

The silent question takes me by surprise, and I automatically shut it down. I don't care how well he'll age, because he'll be in prison. Where he belongs.

My pledge not to think about my new boss and how I could bounce a quarter off his ass lasts about thirty more seconds. Randi sets a bottle of Veuve Clicquot on the table with two glasses.

"Whoa. Where did this come from?" I jerk my gaze from the classic yellow label to her in confusion, because there's no way Lambo's Sports Bar stocks the pricey champagne.

"Bought it special for you because I knew you'd nail that interview. Now tell me, are you going to fuck him?" She slides onto the tall stool across from me with a grin stretching her magenta-slicked lips.

"Are you serious?" I'm overwhelmed with the gesture of generosity from a woman I've known for only a few months. My last living family member, my stepmother, wouldn't even text me congratulations if she knew I'd gotten a new job. She can't be bothered. Something pangs in my chest, and I'm self-aware enough to recognize it as my need for belonging rising to the surface.

My therapist has gotten rich off ferreting out my issues, not the least of which is being the human equivalent of a chameleon for a living without any solid support system now that my dad is gone.

"Of course. You deserve it. The champagne and the fucking," Randi says as she pours the bubbling liquid into both flutes. When she replaces the bottle on the table, she picks up a flute and waits for me to do the same.

My stepmother would turn her nose up at drinking champagne from anything but the finest crystal, but I couldn't care less. *No more shrink issues tonight*, I vow as I lift the glass by the stem. We clink the rims together.

"Congrats, doll."

"Thank you. Seriously, Randi, this is above and beyond."

Randi tips hers back and chugs it while I sip. "Psh, no such thing. That's what friends do. Besides, this shit ain't free, and the price you're paying is *dirt*. Spill. I want to hear all about him. Did he hit on you during the interview? Try to grab your ass? I heard Cannon Freeman is a total *dog*."

I open my mouth to reply, but Randi isn't really ready for an answer yet. Based on my past experience, it's more beneficial to let her have her say without trying to interject. You never know what golden nuggets you'll pick up.

"My friend Tricia said that he barely let her get in the cab before he had his hand up her skirt and finger-fucked her to orgasm within three blocks. Obviously, it was rush hour, and she's an easy come, but still. That's impressive shit." Randi taps her long, dagger-shaped fingernails against the Formica tabletop. Not surprisingly, they match her magenta lips and are tipped with silver glitter.

A silent protest ripples through my brain, like part of me doesn't want to believe that beautiful man is a complete whore. *What the hell?* I couldn't care less if he's a manwhore. It doesn't matter one single bit to me.

I sip my champagne and tell myself more information is better than less, and this will be one more nail in the coffin when I bury him.

I sit back and readjust my position on the hard wooden stool as I prepare to learn more. "Really? Do tell. If my new boss has wandering hands, I need to know."

Randi throws her head back and laughs with enough gusto that I'm worried her tits are going to spill out of her tiny jersey.

"Why is that funny?" I ask, replaying what I just said in my head.

She shoots me a wink. "The laugh isn't for you. That's for the three dicks I've got on the line for tonight. Men love to see a woman laugh. It's like crack for their cocks."

Immediately, I remember what Dominic Casso said to me on the sidewalk, and I shut that line of thought down as fast as humanly possible. *Please, God, tell me that he wasn't looking at me as a potential bed partner. That is just . . . Nope. Nope. Nope. Hell to the nope.*

Randi lifts the champagne bottle to top off both our glasses. "And besides," she says, expertly pouring without a drop hitting the table as she shifts between the two glasses. "It's not his wandering hands you'll have to worry about. He's a dog with a big, wandering dick. He'll never fuck the same pussy twice. I've heard that the last couple years he's had a new bitch almost every night, and they're all begging for more, but he doesn't want anything to do with his own sloppy seconds."

I can't help but wonder if her bending forward until her nipples are practically showing is for the benefit of the eggplants or because she's really planning to tell me a secret. She lowers her voice to a whisper, and I have my answer.

"They line up for him now that they think he could possibly be the next head of the family. Power is the ultimate pussy magnet."

The next head of the family. I don't know where Randi got this much information, but I assume it's from one of those women who didn't get a second shot at the man in question.

It's not difficult to imagine Cannon Freeman strolling through a room packed with women, his hands in the pockets of his tailored suit pants, surveying the offerings. He'd stop in front of one and give her a chin lift and say something like, *"Come on. You're coming with me tonight. All night."*

For some stupid reason, my thighs clench together at the image. The man has enough power and presence to pull it off, regardless of the cheesy line.

"I can see that," I tell her, sipping like the information is nothing but anecdotal.

Randi's sparkling brown eyes snap to my face. "You want to fuck him. Don't deny it. I knew you would." She pumps her fist in the air like she won a prize.

"What? No. Of course not."

I deny it vehemently, even though part of me did consider using seduction to get the information I need, but only one night isn't going to do jack. Cannon Freeman isn't the kind of man who would spill everything in pillow talk after a single killer orgasm. No, he needs to trust me implicitly before he'll tell me anything worthwhile. You don't live this long in a mob family by being stupid or indiscreet.

"Psh. He'd fuck you. Maybe even more than once. God, wouldn't that be the tits? If you were the woman to break the one-night spell?"

I roll my eyes at her. "Like he's Sleeping Beauty waiting for a kiss from the prince?"

"If Sleeping Beauty were a guy with a big ol' dick waiting for the right pussy to fuck twice," Randi says with a laugh. "Damn, that'd be a good story. I should write that shit down."

She untucks her phone from where it's trapped between her black lacy bra and her right boob, and her thumbs fly over the screen as she makes notes.

As soon as she puts it down, I can't help but ask, "Anything else you want to share that you didn't mention before the interview? Anything that'll help me keep my job?"

Randi taps a nail against the side of her phone, and the

glitter flashes in the light of the bar. "I've heard he fucks everyone who works for him, but that's not wildly surprising. How could anyone resist? Hmm . . ."

"How's his relationship with his dad?" I ask, leading her away from the sexual topics that make me want to squirm in my seat.

Randi's eyes widen, and she ducks her head down toward me and the champagne flutes. "Don't say that out loud. Not in public, and for God's sake, not that loud." She scans the bar as if looking for a hit squad coming to kill us.

I lower my voice and lean closer. "It's not a secret, though. At least, I thought that's what you said when I applied for the job."

"It might be the worst-kept secret, but it's not something you wanna be talking about . . . if you know what I mean," Randi whispers.

I know exactly what she means. Because people who get caught digging too close to the Casso family end up six feet under. If they're lucky.

As my celebratory mood fades with that thought, a man comes up behind Randi and covers both shoulders with his hands.

"Watching you over here is killing me, babe. You and your friend want to come join us? We'll show you both a real good time."

The guy is about as tall as Randi is while seated, but she glances down at his hand on her left shoulder—his massive hand—and looks up at him from under her eyelashes. "You're pretty bold for a little guy."

"I ain't little everywhere. Promise."

I avoid the awkwardness of overhearing their flirting by staring down at my almost-empty champagne glass. After about five minutes, I decide my presence is *de trop*.

"I gotta go, Randi. Big day tomorrow with the new job. Thank you so much for the champagne. You're the best."

Randi and her friend both watch me slide off my stool and slip my bag over my shoulder. Once I'm on my feet, he scans me from the top of my blond wig to the toes of my black leather boots.

"You're more than welcome to join us, babe."

I'm five foot five, and I can look him directly in the eye. Not exactly what I would have pegged as Randi's type . . . until I remember that her self-professed type is pretty much everyone.

"Thanks, but I'm heading home." I round the table to slip an arm around Randi's shoulder and give her a halfway hug while avoiding touching her date. "Be safe."

She catches me against her even tighter. "Always. No glove, no love. Talk at you after your first day. Knock 'em dead."

As I walk out of the bar, I feel a sting of remorse that I've forged this friendship with Randi under false pretenses. She's good people. I vow to myself that whatever happens next, none of this will blow back on her.

5

DREW

The next morning, I inhale the moneyed air of the Upper Ten as I cross the threshold into the foyer. Sir No Neck, whose name I don't yet know, is standing in a big-and-tall-collection suit with his arms crossed.

At first, I think it's a casual pose, at least until I see the subtle variation in the lines of his suit. Nope, his arms aren't crossed to look casual. He's probably able to draw two pistols from his discreet shoulder holsters faster than I could duck to miss the bullets.

"Ms. Carson," he says in a voice deeper than the ocean, with Brooklyn vividly coloring his speech. "Welcome to the Upper Ten. If you ever need something, you let me know. I take care of things around here for Mr. Freeman."

"Thank you, Mr. . . ."

"No mister. Just Grice."

Wanting to start insinuating myself with every single person I can, as soon as possible, I hold out my hand. "It's a pleasure to meet you, Grice. I'm Drew. That Ms. Carson business is too formal for me too."

His bearlike paw closes around my proffered hand. "Nah. You're a classy broad. Ms. Carson it is."

As I smile, he gives my hand a shake gentler than I would have expected, and then releases me to open the door behind him.

"Give her hell. She's all bark. You know the type."

"What? Who?" I ask the question, but his attention is already on the next person walking through the entrance into the foyer.

With Grice's cryptic remark on my mind, I step into the Upper Ten and pause to survey the empty lounge.

It's a haven for rich men. Every wingback chair invites a man to sit down and drink a snifter of cognac and smoke a cigar, away from the hustle and bustle of the city streets sixteen stories below us. With its exclusive clientele, members of the Upper Ten don't have to be worried about being bothered, regardless of whether they're famous or notorious.

The tinge of lemon I detected yesterday is even stronger today, which I assume means the housekeeping crew has been through to keep the luxurious space meticulous.

"You're late."

A sharp tone cuts me from behind, and I spin around to face a tall, fit woman with a light brown lob as she stares daggers at me.

"I was supposed to be here at ten, right?"

I glance down at my watch, but forget I took it off because I didn't think a waitress should be wearing an engraved Cartier timepiece without a solid explanation, and *my father gave it to me for graduating summa cum laude from journalism school* would be the absolute worst one to give. I try not to lie about stupid things, so even though I hate not wearing it, it's tucked safely in my drawer at home. But still, I know from my last glance at my cell phone that I'm still at least ten minutes early. After being a reporter for years, I show up early everywhere.

"It's nine forty-seven. All training meetings start at nine thirty, which means you're late. Come on, you've got a lot to learn in a morning." She spins on her shiny black heels and marches toward the panel where Cannon took me for my interview yesterday.

Give her hell. She's all bark. Now I know exactly what Grice was talking about.

I also know that Cannon told me to be here at ten, but I'm not going to argue with the woman, especially since she walked away without introducing herself. I have to assume she's Tanya, the head waitress, which means my new job is going to be *fabulous*.

Stepping quickly to keep up with her as she disappears into the secret door, I slip inside and follow her down the hallway.

"Employee break room is right here." She stops in front of the last door on the left. The one at the end of the hall is closed, and I wonder if the boss is inside.

The thought of seeing Cannon again sends a cavalcade of shivers running up and down my spine. *Those are not shivers of anticipation. They're dread*, I tell myself.

The woman snaps her fingers, and I jerk my chin toward her.

"Pay attention, Carson." She shoves through the door and points to a wall of wooden lockers. "You're locker number seven. Don't lose the key. Cannon hates to break out the bolt cutters."

From her bitchy attitude, it's obvious she doesn't like me. Anyone could figure that out, but I don't know what I did to earn her animosity.

"Got it." I sweep by her, careful to keep a few inches between us, and make my way to locker number seven.

As I'm tucking my purse inside, she produces a set of keys out of her pocket and uses them to unlock a closet on the other wall. She yanks out two pristine white shirts.

"Try these both on. Choose whichever fits best but doesn't leave your tits busting out. That's not what we're here for, get me?"

"Of course."

Her eyes narrow like she's trying to determine whether I'm lying and got this job for the purpose of trying to snag myself a rich man. *If she only knew the truth . . .*

"Do you drink?" The next question out of her mouth surprises me even more.

"Some. A glass of wine with dinner or a cocktail with friends. I've bartended before, so I know my way around if you need backup there—"

She cuts me off with a militant expression. "That's not what I mean. I'm talking about all day, every day. Not just to wind down in the evening."

I shake my head, and whatever she sees on my face must pass inspection.

Nodding, she says, "Good. The last thing we need here is someone slipping behind the bar to take a shot to get through the shift. You ever drink the alcohol here, you're fired. If I catch you snorting anything or popping pills, Cannon will toss you out himself. Understand?"

"Yes. Absolutely. I would never dream of it."

She steps away from the closet, and her features lose some of their aggression. "We'll order you a few more in whatever size you need. I'll be waiting in the bar area for you when you're done. Make it quick."

After she shoves the two hangers at me and I grab them, I

hold my breath until she disappears from the employee break room.

Riiight. She's definitely all bark.

I quickly try on the shirt and choose the larger size just to be safe, because I don't want to misstep any further when it comes to her. With the shirt I was wearing tucked into the locker with my purse, the discarded size hung precisely where it goes in the closet, I straighten my shoulders and head out to face her straight on.

She won't scare me away, no matter how hard she tries.

* * *

THE NEXT HOUR flies by in a blur.

I meet the day-shift bartender, Letty, a cheerful single mom in black slacks, a white shirt, and black vest that I assume is the bartender uniform. It certainly suits her black angled pixie-cut hairstyle and dark brown eyes. She tells me that her evening shift counterpart is Stefano, and that I'll love him. I take her word for it but reserve judgment for when I meet the man with a name straight out of the soap opera my grandma watched up until she died three years ago.

I learn the layout of the club, including which rooms are for cigars and which don't permit smoking. The glassed-in room is referred to as the conservatory, which immediately starts me thinking about Clue and how it was probably Colonel Mustard, with the candlestick.

A rush of the grief I've shoved down so effectively bubbles up with the thought. Dad and I played Clue all the time. And it was always motherfucking Colonel Mustard with the goddamned candlestick.

I promise you'll have justice, Dad. I promise.

Unfortunately, my little jaunt down memory lane earns me a reprimand in the midst of Tanya's spiel on why I'm not allowed to ever leave with a member, which seems to correspond directly to her warning not to choose a shirt that leaves my tits busting out. *As if that would really be an issue.*

"Are you paying attention? Jesus. How is it possible he hired you?" Tanya snaps, although she has yet to introduce herself to me. Then she looks over my shoulder, and immediately, the sour expression that has pinched her features since the minute I walked in morphs into a sweet, welcoming smile. "Hey, Cannon. How are you this morning?"

Instantly, the hair on the back of my neck stands on end. I can feel him walking closer, even though the thick carpet muffles his footsteps. But nothing could mute the sheer magnitude of his presence. I curl my fingers into fists, fighting my unsettling awareness of him.

"Morning, Tanya. Drew." He halts beside me, and I glance up at his carved cheekbones, strong jaw, and intense hazel eyes. "How's the training going?"

I expect Tanya to immediately give him the rundown on how horrible she thinks I am, starting with me allegedly showing up late, which I'm hoping Cannon will then correct her about because he told me to come in at ten. But shockingly, she doesn't.

"Too soon to tell, but I trust your judgment, Boss. You know that." Her gaze clings to Cannon and her fingers flex at her sides, like she wants to reach out to touch him, but won't because they have an audience.

"He fucks everyone who works for him," Randi's voice whispers in my brain. *"It's not his wandering hands you'll have to worry about. He's a dog with a big, wandering dick. He'll never fuck the same pussy twice."*

Oh Lord. I really hope that's not the case, because having

31

my new superior hate me because she's sure the boss is going to try to sleep with me when he won't come back to her bed would be awkward as hell and supremely unhelpful.

"I knew you'd take good care of her. When you're done today, make sure you introduce her to Matteo. He's training her on the inventory this afternoon." Only after he's made the declaration about something that's happening in my life shortly, which no one has bothered to inform me about, does Cannon Freeman turn the full force of his magnetic personality on me.

He stares directly into my eyes, his brow furrowing as though he's trying to see beneath the layers of my makeup.

Good luck. I've got the stuff caked on for a reason.

"You have any questions yet, Drew?"

I have thousands of questions for Cannon, but only two very, very important ones—why did the Casso family order my father's death, and who did it? But of course, I can't ask them.

"No questions." I lie with a cheerful smile on my face that's as fake as my name. "Tanya is doing a great job. I'm excited to shadow her today and learn the ropes firsthand."

I expect to hear a pissed huff from Tanya, but her expression is one of pure worship.

Oh, good Lord. This is so weird.

"Perfect." Cannon's gaze tracks over my uniform shirt. "I'm glad. I don't like to make hiring mistakes. No good comes of that. I'll catch up with you later to answer any questions Tanya and Matteo can't."

Even after his eyes leave me and he takes a half step back, clearly intending to leave us, his scrutiny remains like tiny pinpricks all over my skin. I've never been this hyperaware of a man before, and I don't know what to do about it.

"I have a question for you," Tanya says with honey dripping from her tone before he can turn.

It's impressive that the edges of her phony smile aren't wearing thin already. It has to be a lot of effort for her to pretend this effectively when only moments ago she could have won a contest for superbitch.

"Can we talk about it in your office after the lunch rush?" she asks. "I'm sure you know what I want to discuss."

Did her lashes just flutter? Lord, she's got it bad.

"Not today, Tanya. I'm busy." Cannon's tone shifts from easy to harsh in a heartbeat.

Tanya bites down on her lower lip, as if holding in a protest, but says nothing further as Cannon disappears into the hidden hallway. As soon as he's gone, her chin rises an inch and she glares down her nose at me.

"Don't make me look bad while we're working, or you'll be out on your ass tomorrow."

And . . . superbitch is back.

6

DREW

For the next two hours, I shadow Tanya as she works the room, efficiently moving from table to table, taking orders and chatting amiably with the club members.

For all that she's a complete bitch to me, I have to admit she handles the members with laughable ease. Apparently, I'm not the only chameleon in this place.

We move to a new table, and her bright smile, just a few watts dimmer than the one she graced Cannon with, lands on a celebrity actor who has a reputation for being extremely private. I remember reading once that he doesn't have any social media accounts, and he once told a journalist that he only owed the public his performances, not his soul. Of course, the media just tried harder to hound him for interviews after that—an assignment that I turned down because digging through his trash to find out what he was really up to wasn't of interest to me.

"Hey, Tanya. Good to see you," Silas Bohannon says as he lowers the newspaper he's reading.

"You too, Silas. You drinking, eating, or just smoking

today?" she asks, opting to not introduce me as the new trainee, like she has for every other table.

Hmmm. I can't help but wonder why not. Territorial? The rest of the men we've served over the last two hours were businessmen and politicians, and Silas Bohannon is our first celebrity.

"Eating and smoking. Although my trainer keeps telling me I have to turn in my humidor key." He shakes his head with a smile. "Too bad he doesn't always get what he wants."

"Absolutely. What's life without a few vices?" Tanya leans forward to remove the wineglass from the place setting in front of him.

Instead of responding to her question, he cranes his neck to get a better view of me. "Who's your friend?"

Almost as though she forgot I was standing next to her, Tanya glances over her shoulder. "Oh, this is Drew. She's learning the ropes. First day."

"Nice to meet you, Drew." His gaze narrows on me. "Have we met before? You look familiar."

My stomach instantly twists into a web of knots, but I school my reaction to casual confusion. There's no way he can recognize me, even if he's seen me on TV before. I knew walking into this job that I'd be facing a crowd of the most elite members of the city, some of whom I've interviewed before, and I took great pains to change my appearance as much as possible. I'm not just a chameleon, I'm a damn good one.

"I would definitely remember if we'd met before, sir. I can safely say we haven't." I keep my tone friendly, deliberately injecting a hint of star-struck, but keep my hands firmly clamped together by my waist.

Silas scans me closer. "Are you sure? You haven't been auditioning in town lately?"

Thankfully, Tanya's booming laughter saves me from coming up with an answer. "She's no actress, Silas. Trust me. We're still trying to see if she can hack it as a waitress."

How the hell Tanya feels like she knows me well enough to make that statement, I have no idea, but I'm ready to hug her for it.

To firmly close out this line of questioning, I add, "I'm just one of those people with a familiar face. It's an honor to meet you, sir. I'm happy to take your order when you've made a lunch selection."

Tanya's laughter fades to a pointed look. She's probably pissed that I'm stepping on her toes by offering to take his order, but I'll risk her anger to kill this conversation.

"Salmon Caesar salad, no cheese, no croutons, dressing on the side. Basically, boring as fuck, but that's the price of playing a superhero, I guess. A bottle of still water as well, please."

"I can't wait to see the movie," Tanya says, regaining control of the encounter. "We'll have your lunch out to you in a moment, and I'll let Matteo know that you'll be using your regular room when you finish eating."

Silas's attention still splits between us. "Thanks, ladies. Nice to meet you, Drew."

As we walk away from the table, Tanya makes a beeline for the kitchen, not stopping until we slip inside the doors. She turns her icy blue eyes on me as her fingers latch onto my wrist like a cuff. "Whatever you're thinking right now, stop. This is one of the only places in this city where Silas can escape from the fawning fans, not another place where he has to be *on*."

Everything in me wants to protest that I don't give a fuck about Silas Bohannon, but that would only invite more questions.

"Understood?"

Tanya's gaze is sharp enough to wound as her nails dig into my skin. And I know it's now or never, if I want to be treated with even a modicum of respect by this woman.

"I don't know what the hell your problem is with me, Tanya, but I'm here to work. Nothing else. Now I'm asking you respectfully to remove your hand from my person before I make you." My stone-cold tone leaves absolutely no question about how serious I am.

With a huff and gritted teeth, Tanya drops my wrist. "You're here because you want something this place can offer. That's why they all try to get jobs here. Easy access to rich men to pay for your life in exchange for a little suck and fuck in return. Or maybe you're out to try to get Cannon's attention. Well, guess what? He's off-limits. Won't fucking touch you, even if you laid out naked on the bar and spread your legs for him. Got it?"

Squaring my shoulders, I stare her down with the colored contacts turning my eyes from aquamarine to brown, and lie my ass off. "I'm here for a steady job and paycheck. That's it. End of story."

Tanya's eyes narrow until her glare is piercing enough to impale. "I don't believe you."

"I don't care what you believe, but here's one thing you can take to the bank—I don't want your boss in my bed. There's no need to piss on your territory to scare me off. Now, if you're done lifting your leg, let's get back to work." I straighten my shirt cuffs and lift my chin high, all under Tanya's continued glare.

"I don't like you, and that means you won't last. Now go place Silas's order with the chef and don't fuck it up. Actually, do. Because I'd love to have a reason to fire you on your first day."

When she stomps out of the kitchen, all I can think is *Well, hell. I probably should have handled that better.*

THANKFULLY, training with Matteo, an older Cuban man with an inky black widow's peak and gray frosting his temples, who I learn is Letty's uncle, takes me away from Tanya's rancid attitude for the next three hours. Inside the large glassed-in room, he assesses my knowledge of cigars, which he deems adequate, and I have my father to thank for that.

Dad always indulged himself with a smoke on the back deck at night after dinner. That's when he lit a fire in me about becoming an investigative reporter, and taught me the things he didn't think young journalists knew well enough when they got started in his world.

How to be objective. How to look for the right perspective. How to be unbiased and always focus on finding the truth, not only looking for evidence that supported the conclusion you thought would be right. Keeping an open mind when your investigation took a different turn than you expected, because there was nothing worse than twisting the facts into something other than what they were.

Then he'd tap the ashes in the ceramic dish he hid from Mother and press one finger to his lips to remind me that this was all our secret. As if I'd ever tattle on my old man. No, I soaked up every word out of his mouth like a sponge. There was never a chance of any other career for me. I wanted to grow up to be just like Dad.

"Before we wrap things up, we must talk about the most difficult and yet simple part of your job."

Dragging myself back to the present and away from those

cherished memories, I lift my gaze from the lid of a box of Cohibas to meet Matteo's ruddy-cheeked expression.

"What's that?"

"The art of the upsell." He waves his hand at the left side of the room, where glass-fronted humidors contain box after box of cigars on angled shelves that allow for maximum visibility. "That is where we keep our most expensive inventory, each cigar more precious than the last. Make no mistake, if the fire alarm were ever to sound, we get the cigars out before we leave. They are like my children, you see?" His voice carries the exotic lilt of Cuba as he waves with a flourish at the boxes.

I take a step closer and scan the labels. "Which one is the most expensive?"

He shifts to the center glass case and points at a box cradling the artfully rolled cigars. "It is not necessarily the brand or the name that makes a cigar expensive. Sometimes it is the story behind it, and the rarity. These were made by Fidel Castro's personal cigar roller. They are nearly impossible to find anymore."

"That's impressive. How much are they?"

"We charge ten thousand per stick. It pairs nicely with the five-thousand-dollar-per-shot cognac from the French Revolution, or the Pappy Van Winkle." Matteo turns to me with a smile. "And your job is to entice patrons to amplify their experience here with the most exclusive of everything. Other than privacy and comfort, that is our most valuable offering."

He runs through the other expensive cigars I'm supposed to upsell—the Gurkha Black Dragons, stored in their hand-crafted camel-bone boxes that are around twelve hundred dollars per stick or over a hundred grand for the box. The Arturo Fuente Opus X, which now seems to be a great deal at over thirty thousand per box. The Cohiba Behikes are practically bargain priced in my mind because they're under twenty grand per box. The price scale continues downward with cigars ranging in price from hundreds of dollars for one to merely fifty.

I commit every word to memory, which is a habit I honed while interviewing on the off chance my recorder would fail or the recording turned out muffled.

An hour later, a tap on the glass catches my attention. I expect to see Tanya summoning me, but Cannon stands there watching us.

How long has he been there, and how didn't I notice?

I blame it on the ventilation system, that's louder in here due to the particular needs of the cigars.

With a friendly expression, Matteo waves to the boss. "My time is up, Drew. Do not hesitate to come back for more lessons. The more you know about the cigars and their stories, the more effective you will be at your job."

He has no way of knowing that the only reason I want to be effective at my job is to find out what the man on the other side of the glass knows. And if I do it right, he never will.

I hold out a hand, and Matteo shakes it. "Thank you for your time and expertise, sir. It was a pleasure."

"Don't be a stranger. And good luck with Tanya. She's not an easy one, but she is loyal once you are part of her circle."

Yet another warning about Tanya. Interesting.

I move to the door Cannon is opening, and note his features are tight rather than relaxed like they were when I saw him this morning.

My first thought is—*he knows.* But that's impossible. Ariel is one of the best hackers in the world. The mob doesn't have anyone who could drill through the false identity she created for me.

With my heart hammering, I step out of the humidor room and wait for him to speak.

"I need to talk to you in my office."

7

DREW

*B*eing called into my boss's office on my first day, especially when he's wearing an unreadable expression, isn't a good sign for a regular employee.

And for someone like me? It's a one-way ticket to terror.

The rational part of my brain is hoping this is simply a formality following the end of my shift. *Or maybe Tanya said something to try to get me fired?* Either of those are vastly preferable to the only other alternative I can think of right now—that someone recognized me . . . like Silas Bohannon.

With a lump in my throat, I focus on my steps, keeping them even and at pace with Cannon's as I follow him to his office. Once we're inside, he closes the door.

"Sit."

I'm tempted to glance behind me, but I err on the side of obeying his order in silence. He doesn't take a seat behind his desk until I've lowered myself into the leather club chair.

"Are you going to quit?" Cannon's question catches me completely off guard.

"What?"

"Are you going to quit today?" He speaks slower this time,

a current of tension underlying each perfectly enunciated word. His hazel eyes sizzle and snap, like he's daring me to lie to him.

Already have, Cannon. Will definitely continue.

My shoulder blades press into the padding of the leather back as he brushes a hand through his dark brown hair in a frustrated move.

"I wasn't planning on it," I reply carefully. "Why would you ask that?" The confusion in my tone is totally genuine.

"Because Tanya seems to think you won't be able to hack it. She's laying money on the fact that you won't show up tomorrow."

Heat, a direct result of the anger burning deep in my chest, floods my system. I clamp my teeth together to stop the words dying to spring forth and take a deep breath instead.

Cannon watches me closely, as if he's observing every fleeting emotion I'm trying not to show on my face while I prepare a response that isn't *your head waitress is a massive bitch who needs an attitude adjustment.*

Apparently, Cannon is tired of waiting for me to reply, because he says, "She's going to try to make you quit. I would've warned you, but that's not how things work here. If you can't handle her, you can't handle the job."

"I can handle her and the job, *sir.*" The emphasis on the last word comes through my clenched teeth.

Cannon leans back in his chair and crosses one ankle over a knee. "You're stone cold, aren't you, Drew? That's a quality I don't often see in women around here."

"You don't have many women around here, from what I've noticed," I say, not sure what kind of reaction he's fishing for.

"Women aren't allowed to apply for membership to the

43

Upper Ten. They're only allowed in the club for special occasions, which take place two or three times per year. But that's not what I'm talking about, and you know it."

I lift my chin in challenge that comes naturally to me. I don't know what his purpose is, but I'm not losing this job as soon as I got it. *I need to be here.* "What are we talking about, sir?"

"Cut the *sir* shit. My name is Cannon. No one here has ever called me sir and meant it with respect, so no one says it. Understand?"

"Yes, s—. I mean yes, Cannon."

He uncrosses his ankle and shifts forward in his chair to lean his elbows on the desk. "Good. Because with brass balls like you've got, you'll do well here. Win Tanya over, and you'll do even better. It's not your fault she hates you. She'd hate anyone in your position. That's on me, but I'm not going to fix it for you."

What a dick. He knows she's pissed at him for their one-night stand, and he's going to let her take it out on me? Asshole move.

My chin goes higher. "I'm not sleeping with you. I'm sure as soon as she understands *that*, we won't have a problem."

Cannon's head jerks back and his eyes narrow on me.

Fuck. I shouldn't have said that. If I was considering seduction as a last resort for information, I've jacked it up royally.

Cannon's chest puffs out as his gaze bores into me. "Says who?" The words come out quiet and dangerous, and the heat that was rushing through my system from anger pools between my legs.

No. No. Seduction is a last resort. Not a first choice. I dump a mental bucket of ice water on my unruly lady parts and reinforce my bravado.

"Me. I don't care if you screw every woman who walks in this door, but I won't be on the list."

A predatory smile stretches over his face, and holy hell, if that isn't a good look for him, then I don't know what is. My panties are a lost cause as his green and-amber gaze catches and holds mine.

"Interesting." He breaks our stare to push a piece of paper across the desk toward me, and when he looks up, there's no trace of the intensity that was there a second ago.

Whoa. It's like he changed his mask. The trick is impressive to me, wildly so, given my chosen occupation.

"In the meantime," he says as I glance down at the paper, "here's your schedule. You're on days until your training is finished and we'll ease you into the evenings. Club is open until two a.m., unless we have a special request from a member, in which case, we will stay open all night, if necessary."

"Doesn't the State Liquor Authority have a problem with that?" As soon as the question is out, I know it's a stupid one. *This is a mob establishment.*

A smirk tugs at the corners of Cannon's mouth. "You'll find, Drew, that many rules that apply to everyone else don't apply to us. But if you're really concerned, the chairman of the SLA should be in tomorrow night. He enjoys his Cohibas." He rises and waves toward the door. "You can show yourself out."

8

DREW

*D*ay two moves along much like day one, except I arrive fifteen minutes before the appointed time printed on my schedule. There are four pressed white shirts hanging on the door of my locker, and I change into one after stowing my bag. I'm on the floor a full five minutes before Tanya walks in the door.

If I thought she was in fine form yesterday, today's mood is even worse. She barely speaks to me. I follow her silently, memorizing orders, and even correcting her once when she relays them to the kitchen staff. It doesn't win me any favors.

At four, she has to leave to run an errand and appoints Letty my watchdog for the hour she'll be gone. Cannon is nowhere to be found, and I'm starting to wonder if my grand idea of infiltrating the Casso family through one of their legitimate operations is going to work.

Be patient. It will work. Persevere.

Perseverance is another trait learned from my father. He had a quiet sense of power coupled with unrelenting determination. You might think he'd abandoned a problem or investigation, but he never did. He'd continue wearing away at it like water through the Grand Canyon.

"Good investigative journalists aren't always flashy and bold. There's a lot to be said for subtlety."

Subtlety. I can do that. Well, maybe after I figure out which pricey cigar is shoved so far up Tanya's ass that she can barely stand to look at me.

"What's her deal?" I ask Letty as she sets a vodka martini on the tray of drinks she and I are serving to a rapper and a record exec in the corner.

"Whose deal?" Letty looks around, as if there's another woman here other than the two of us.

"Tanya's."

Before she can answer me, Grice appears at my side.

"Need one of you to take the door for a minute. Boss is gone, Matteo's busy, and Tanya's not back yet. Shouldn't be anyone coming in, though. I gotta run down to meet a delivery."

"Tanya will kill us all if I let Drew serve tables by herself." Letty glances from Grice to me. "You comfortable handling the door?"

Like any new employee, I give her an energetic nod. "Sure. Of course. Whatever you need."

"Thanks, Ms. Carson."

I follow Grice to the entrance, and he points to the corner where he usually stands.

"Hang out here. I'll be back in five. Members need a keycard to get up to this floor without an escort, but hopefully no one shows while I'm gone."

"I can handle it, Grice. Do what you need to do."

The big man exits the club, and I stand sentry, wishing he'd left me guarding a room I could scour for papers that might bring me one step closer to answers. Unfortunately, the foyer, with its high ceiling, heavy brass light fixtures, grandfather clock, and carefully tended fiddle-leaf fig tree offer none. Why I know it's a fiddle-leaf fig can be attributed to my stepmother, who is almost as particular about her indoor plants as she is about her cosmetic surgeries. She currently looks forty-five, but if she's not careful, she'll look like a newly face-lifted Joan Rivers in a few years.

The grandfather clock ticks over three minutes before the door opens. I smile, expecting to see Grice returning more quickly than expected, but it's not. Instead, it's a man with a confident stride.

"Nice to see they've upgraded the help around here to a pretty girl instead of that goon who usually watches the door. How's it going, honey?"

Something about this guy immediately rubs me the wrong way, and his leer makes me feel like I need to shower.

"Grice will be back in a few minutes. I'm helping him out."

The man steps toward me and attempts to drop his voice lower, but the pitch is still too high for his purpose. "How about I let you help me out instead? You're a little old for my taste, but I'd still give you a good ride."

All of my creeper alerts are going crazy, but instead of saying *Ew, gross. Never fucking ever*, I smile and reply politely. "I'm sorry, sir. That's against club policy."

I stretch out a hand to wave him toward the club, but Tanya enters the main door.

The man spins around to look at Tanya, and her face goes white.

"What are you doing here?" she asks him quickly before her gaze darts to me. "And where the hell is Grice?"

"He's meeting a delivery," I say, wondering what I'm

missing here. "He left me in charge of the door for five minutes."

"Fucking hell."

The man's smooth, affable smile disappears. "Where's my favorite little bitch? You know you can't keep her from me."

"None of your goddamned business," Tanya snaps. "And I sure as hell can."

What the hell is going on here? My attention jumps between them as Tanya's expression twists with murderous rage.

He gives her a smug smile. "I'm gonna find her. You can't babysit her all the time. She's an adult, and she makes her own decisions."

Tanya's fingers curl into claws. "You come near her again, and I'll fucking kill you myself."

The man charges at her, moving faster than I would have thought possible. In a second, he has Tanya pressed up against the wall, his hands on her shoulders, ready to shake her.

"Big words for a bitch with no backup—"

The interior door flies open.

"Back the fuck away from her before I rip your hands off and give them to the hookers down the street so they can jerk off their johns." Cannon's quiet and deadly voice issues the threat from just behind me.

The man, who clearly values his hands more than getting information out of Tanya, releases her and backs away. "You think you're hot shit, Freeman? I don't give a fuck who your father is. My boss will have my back if you touch me. You want to start a war? Bring it."

"You're the one about to fuck up months of negotiations, and there's no way anyone is going to blame me for taking you out. I'm only going to say this one more time, Donny. Get the fuck out of this club and never come back, including with your boss." Cannon stalks toward him, stopping only when the tips of his Italian shoes are inches from Donny's. "Because the next time you set foot on my property, you leave in a body bag. Do you understand me?"

Donny's face turns ashen and beads of sweat glisten on his temples as he backs up toward the door. As soon as his fingers wrap around the door handle, his lip curls. "You're going to regret this."

"No. I won't. Just like I won't regret sending you six feet under. Now give me the keycard you stole to get up here and move your ass. I don't want to breathe the same air as you."

Donny yanks a plastic card from his pocket before flinging it at Cannon with bared teeth. Then he slips out the door, and a heavy shroud of silence settles over all three of us. No one speaks for a few beats, at least, not until Tanya rushes to Cannon and throws herself into his arms.

"Thank you. Thank you so much. I know that wasn't how things are supposed to go. I didn't think he'd have the balls to try to get in here without . . ." Tanya trails off as Cannon's arms wrap around her, and I'm still trying to figure out exactly what I just witnessed.

Which rival mob family does that guy work for? Could this somehow help my case?

Tanya shudders against Cannon, and my mind splits off down another avenue, even as I'm thinking about my investigation.

They look pretty damn cozy together.

He tucks her hair behind her ears and drops his voice to a low murmur. "It's okay, sweetheart. We'll deal with this. I promised you that once, and I meant it."

Sweetheart. He called her sweetheart. That's enough to prove the suspicion I had about them being together, which should be gratifying. Instead, a green-eyed, clawing monster rears her ugly head from the pettiest part of my soul.

Under normal circumstances, I'd laugh it off as no big deal, but I'm frozen in the entryway, hating him and hating myself at the same time.

I can't be jealous. If I'm jealous . . . that means I . . . I don't even want to put it into words, but my brain can't be stopped.

I want him.

A chill sweeps over me, unleashing goose bumps that spread across every inch of my exposed skin. *I can't want him. I—*

"I hate him." Tanya's rough whisper is barely loud enough for me to hear, but I take a wobbly step back because she steals the words right out of my brain.

I'm supposed to hate Cannon Freeman.

"Shh. I know. We all hate that bastard."

Tanya snuffles and looks up at Cannon from beneath her lashes in a move I've seen Randi use. A move deliberately intended to entice. "Thank you. I appreciate you coming to my rescue."

Part of me wants to shrink away because now I'm intruding on a too-intimate scene, but I can't slip out of the foyer without attracting their attention.

Thankfully, the entrance door swings open again. Cannon quickly releases Tanya and steps away from her, leaving the woman staring at him with longing.

"What'd I miss?" Grice's gaze scans the room, and his free hand goes for his gun while he balances a box on his other.

"Donny Linetti," Cannon says, infusing the man's name with disgust.

"Fuck." Grice looks to me. "I'm sorry, Ms. Carson. Didn't think he'd have the balls to try something like that."

"It's—" I start to speak, but Cannon cuts me off.

"He could've been watching the building. I'll be in my office, doing a full security review. Perfect fucking timing before tonight."

Cannon sweeps around me, jamming one hand in his pocket as he reaches for the interior door with the other. Without another word to any of us, he disappears inside the Upper Ten.

"What does he mean, perfect timing before tonight?"

Tanya's blue gaze ices over. "Don't ask questions above your pay grade." She glances down to check her watch. "You're off in two hours. Make sure every glass is clean before you go. I don't need you anymore today."

Tanya disappears through the door as if she's chasing after Cannon, but not without nearly knocking her shoulder into mine.

Fabulous. She hates me even more now. As soon as she's gone, I'm left with a feeling of foreboding I can't shake.

"Sorry for putting you in that situation, Ms. Carson. Never again," Grice says.

"Don't worry about it. How could you have known?" I give him a small smile and head back inside, prepared to wash every glass and make sure they're spotless before I head home for the night.

And I add Donny Linetti, clearly a mob player, to my list of people to research.

9

DREW

*a*s soon as my fingers close around the straps of my bag, I know I'm not alone in the break room. Carefully, like the hair on my neck isn't standing on end, I turn around to see Cannon, the man I am definitely not jealous over, standing in the doorway.

How does he move so quietly? I'm not sure I want an answer to that question, because it probably has to do with things that would add to the prison sentence he's going to get. *Why wouldn't I want to add to his prison sentence?*

"I need you to stay and pull a double. I wouldn't ask it of you normally, especially not on your second day, but I need you tonight. Late-shift waitress isn't coming in. Tanya's staying too."

I remember what he said earlier about the security review being "perfect fucking timing before tonight," which Tanya immediately said was above my pay grade.

This could be the break I need in my investigation.

"Absolutely, sir. Whatever you need." I lower my bag back into the locker as he catalogs every facet of my appearance.

"What did I tell you about the *sir* bullshit?"

"Sorry, s—. Sorry, Cannon. Old habits."

His assessing stare makes me feel like I'm under CIA scrutiny for a lie detector test. Unsettled, yet determined to beat the damn machine.

"You're a drink runner for Tanya," he says, his jaw set in a hard line. "She'll take the orders and give them to Stefano. You bring them out to the tables. It'll be good for you to see how busy we can get in the evenings. This'll be your shift eventually."

"Sounds great," I say, targeting the enthusiasm behind my words specifically to hit the *excited but somewhat nervous new employee* level.

His gaze moves over my face and stops at my hairline. *Shit. Is my wig slipping?*

"Something's not right."

My stomach drops to the green-and-gold-striped carpet beneath my feet. *No. This can't be happening. Not before I learn* anything *helpful.* Visions of my feet being cemented into five-gallon buckets before I'm tossed into the East River assail me as Cannon comes closer.

Stay cool. Act cool. Be cool. I repeat my mantra. *No one can prove I'm lying if I never admit it.* People underestimate the power of deception all the damn time.

"I'm not sure what you mean," I say with a casual, yet politely confused tone, hoping to find out what he thinks is wrong.

"Your uniform."

A rush of relief sweeps through me, but I still glance down at my tailored white shirt with bewilderment. "This is what Tanya told me to wear."

"For day. For night you need a vest and tie. Hold on."

He shoves a hand into his pocket, and the lights catch on a flash of silver keys that jangle as he opens the closet from which Tanya produced the shirts yesterday. Cannon yanks out hangers covered in a clear plastic dry-cleaning bag and offers them to me.

"These vests should fit you. Hell, probably better than they fit her." He murmurs the last bit with a shake of his head.

"Who?"

He shoves the clothing toward me, and I rush to take it. My fingers slide against his, and a spark of heat passes between us.

Cannon's brow furrows as his eyes lock on mine. "Doesn't matter. Take a half-hour break if you want now. You're going to be busy tonight."

He backs toward the door, and I can't help but wonder what the hell just happened in here . . . and whose clothes I'm going to be wearing for my next shift. A check in the mirror shows me that there wasn't a damn thing wrong with my wig placement either.

So, why does he keep looking at me like that?

FOR THE NEXT SEVERAL HOURS, I run drinks to what seems like every upper-class New Yorker. Famous men, notorious men, men who have been on the cover of *Forbes* and *Time Magazine*.

As I deliver thousand-dollar glasses of cognac and catch glimpses of the labels of some of the most expensive cigars from Matteo's inventory, I play a game to keep my attention sharp—attempt to tally the net worth of the people present tonight. I stall out when I try to add the geeky guy whose portrait was in stipple format on the front page of the *Wall*

Street Journal last week. *Did they say he was worth six billion or sixteen billion after his IPO?*

I lose track of time and start to droop. I've been here for almost twelve hours, and I haven't eaten all day. I load my tray with another round of drinks for the table I've labeled *Revenge of the Nerds*, and my stomach growls with the intensity of a pride of lions. Of course, Cannon appears at my side to hear it.

"I should've told you to get some food in the kitchen earlier. Do that now. I need you focused and helping to clear out the tables before midnight."

It might be my fatigue, or maybe the fact that I'm pretty sure I'm light-headed from lack of food, but I stare at him in confusion.

"Doesn't the club close at two?"

The muscle in Cannon's jaw tightens as he rebuttons his suit jacket and scans the club floor. Everything about him screams calm, collected, and completely in control. "Not tonight."

I'm not stupid. There's something big going down, and I'd bet a shred of my soul that it's mob business, especially given his comments about Donny Linetti's appearance earlier. Just the reminder that I might be one step closer to finding answers *tonight* sends a charge through my body like I've mainlined Red Bull.

"Whatever you need, Cannon. I'm here to help."

He scans my appearance, seeming to approve of my uniform, which actually does fit well. Then his gaze narrows on my face, and I get the sense that once again, he's trying to see inside my head, which would be catastrophic to my longevity.

"Important guests will be arriving at midnight. Don't

speak to any of them. Tanya will show them into the conclave."

"The conclave?"

He gives me a short nod, and a sweep of dark hair dips over his forehead. "It's the carved wooden door to the right of the conservatory. Don't go inside."

"Then . . . what do you want me to do if I can't speak to anyone or go inside the room where people need to be served?" I ask, rocking back on my heels.

"Whatever Tanya tells you to do." A buzzing sound comes from his pocket, and he tenses. "I have to go. Don't fuck up anything tonight."

As he walks away, I feel like he leaves behind unsaid words hanging in the air. *Your life depends on it.*

A raft of shivers rips down my spine. *Like someone just walked over my grave.* I straighten my shoulders and pull myself together.

Tonight's the night. Time to get down to business.

10

DREW

*T*he Italians have arrived. It's midnight, and the club was silent for a whole fifteen minutes before a contingent of men swept through the door. Caught out in the open, near the bar where I just finished putting away clean glasses, I smile and do my best Vanna White impression. My arm gracefully extends outward, in a silent gesture that they should continue forward toward the carved door where Tanya is putting the finishing touches on the room for the meeting.

"They're scaling up around here," one of them says as he walks by me. He appears to be the youngest of the bunch and has slicked-back black hair.

His leer leaves me feeling like Donny's did earlier, like I got sprayed with gutter slime, but my smile never wavers.

Four men file into the conclave—two important guests and a pair who are obviously bodyguards. Once they're out of sight, I hurry to Stefano and the bar that now feels like safety, regardless of the fact that I met the man only a few hours ago. His tall, broad-shouldered form is nearly as big as Grice's, but instead of being bald like the younger security guard, his snow-white hair is styled in a spiky fashion. He wears black slacks, a white shirt, and a black vest and tie, which is the masculine version of what I wear.

"Why am I getting the impression that Cannon told me not to talk to them for my safety and not because he was worried about me embarrassing him and the club?" I whisper.

Stefano pauses polishing an already spotless glass behind the bar. "Because he did. You don't want the Rossettis to remember you."

Oh my God. That's who they are.

The Rossettis. The Cassos' number-one rival crime family in the city. I know the name, but since I've spent almost all my time digging exclusively into the Cassos, I don't know as many details as I'd like.

"The Rossettis?" I hook my thumbs in the pockets of my vest as I try to casually pump Stefano for more information while pretending I've never heard of them. Meanwhile, my brain is going crazy.

Holy shit. This meeting is a huge fucking deal. My research showed that these two families have been mortal enemies for decades. Many suspected but unconfirmed incidents, both offensive and retaliatory, have been linked to both families.

Stefano's brows go up. "Giancarlo and his son, GTR? You've never heard of them?"

I shake my head, playing dumb.

His shocked expression tells me I'm doing a bang-up job. "It's probably good you haven't, especially GTR. But if you ever see him coming, you cross the street."

I open my mouth, planning to ask follow-up questions, but before I can gather my thoughts, Grice opens the door and four more men file in, led by Dominic Casso himself.

A whirlpool of unease threatens to sweep me under as I

track his movements. Cannon meets his father in the middle of the club and speaks loudly enough for me to overhear from the bar.

"They're here."

Dom's bodyguards, the same ones from the sidewalk, stop behind him as he speaks to the son he's never publicly acknowledged, according to the insight I gleaned from Randi and my own research.

"Of course they are. You think I'd show up before them?" Dom shoves a hand in his suit pants and jangles some change.

"I'm surprised they showed at all."

"Even Giancarlo Rossetti wouldn't dare snub me by refusing an invite to meet."

But why are they meeting now? I desperately want to know the answer to that question, but of course, Dom doesn't cover that topic. He'd probably need to be in a room swept for bugs and barricaded with steel doors and an escape route from the Feds before spilling secrets like that.

Stefano clinks two glasses together as he replaces the spotless one on the rack, and Dom, his bodyguards, and Cannon all look our way.

A flash of recognition sweeps across Dom's face as he sees me standing at the bar.

"Drew." His tone softens when he says my name, carrying none of the harshness he used when speaking to his son. "What are the odds? You still laughing, pretty girl?"

Cannon's attention cuts between me and his father as a wave of fire washes up my face.

I have to be bright red. Not wanting to disobey Cannon's orders of *don't speak*, I paste a bright smile on my face that is as fake as my name. I just hope nobody else can tell how edgy Dom's presence makes me.

Thankfully, Dom doesn't need an answer from me, and he looks to his son. "You didn't tell me you hired a new waitress."

Cannon's posture turns rigid. "Unless you have an issue with how I run this club, you don't need to know the details. We should go. They're waiting." He takes a step toward the conclave, but Dom doesn't move.

"They can wait. I want to know how Drew is doing." Dom glances at Cannon. "Did you know she and I met the other day?" The older man's steel-colored eyebrow rises as he smiles and walks toward me. "I wondered how I'd find you again, and here you are. Just as pretty as ever."

My spine couldn't be any straighter if someone had strapped titanium rods to my back. My tongue is stuck to the roof of my mouth, because Dom's interest is apparent for all to see.

Now this is awkward as hell. I came with the plan to possibly seduce the son, not get hit on by the father. Even though I know, realistically, getting close to Dominic Casso could get me my answers quicker, I can't do it.

My lungs burn, and I realize I've forgotten to breathe. I quickly suck in oxygen as unobtrusively as possible and try to think of something to say that isn't going to piss Cannon off more than the hard lines of his jaw indicate he already is.

"We haven't been properly introduced." He holds out a hand with heavy gold rings on three fingers. "Dominic Casso."

My teeth clamp down on the inside of my mouth, and I'm terrified of what's going to come out of it next if I don't get my shit together.

Stay cool. Act cool. Be cool.

After repeating my mantra and gathering myself, I slide my hand into his. "Drew Carson."

"Carson. I don't know any Carsons . . . anymore."

Oh good Lord, does that mean the Carsons he knew are all dead?

"Well, you do now," I manage to say in a cool, collected tone.

"It's a pleasure." His gaze sweeps down the front of my uniform shirt and tie. "But you aren't meant to wear a tie, sweetheart. Dresses. Red ones. That's what you need."

"She's a waitress. They don't wear red dresses, sir. Besides, the Rossettis are waiting, and we should go."

Cannon speaks from behind Dom. I can practically hear him grinding his teeth through the entire exchange because I'm wasting their time when they should be meeting with their rivals right now.

But Dom doesn't seem to care about being late, and he doesn't spare a glance at his son. No, his complete attention is firmly fixed on me, and so intently that I feel like he's memorizing every plane and angle of my face as he tilts his head. Through it all, he keeps his unrelenting grip on my hand.

"When I get done here, Drew, you and I are going to get to know each other a little better."

Someone might as well have dumped a bucket of ice water down the back of my shirt, because it takes everything in me not to tremble at his statement.

Fuck. Me. This. Is. Bad.

"I need a Pappy Van Winkle and a Macallan neat," Tanya says, breaking the silent spell holding me captive.

Thankfully, Dom's gaze swings over to her and he releases my hand. "Tanya. You're looking good. You keeping your sister in line?"

As soon as I'm free, I shrink back two nearly imperceptible steps, and for a reason I will never understand, I glance at Cannon. His darkened gaze drills into me.

Fuck. Now he looks like he wants to kill me. *What was I supposed to do?* No one trained me for the situation where I'd have to fend off advances from a mob boss.

"Drew, take your break in the kitchen. You need to eat."

At midnight? He's trying to feed me again at midnight?

Dom's chest bounces and falls with laughter, and I have a feeling it has nothing to do with whatever Tanya is saying right now. He knows his son wants to keep me clear of him, and I'm praying to whoever will listen that it won't make Dom even more persistent. Because he's a man, and they always want what they can't have.

"Yes, sir." I slip away from the bar and make a beeline to the kitchen, kicking myself for calling him sir again. Then again, that's the least of my problems right now as three sets of eyes follow me until I disappear behind the swinging wooden doors.

Hell. What do I do now?

11

CANNON

I can barely concentrate on the meeting, because I'm fucking seething. I know what it looks like when Dom's picking out a new mistress, and he's giving every indication that Drew is the next woman to fill that role.

Who knows what the fuck happened to Elisha, the last piece of arm candy he paraded around. Actually, nothing has probably happened to her—yet. If Dom thinks he has Drew on the line, he'll send Elisha packing to Europe with access to a bank account that'll last her the rest of her life, so long as she never sets foot in New York again.

But he's not fucking doing that with Drew. Not a goddamned chance in hell. It doesn't matter that I'm not ready to dive into the reasons behind my rage over the idea yet either.

This isn't the first time Dom has taken an interest in a woman who he shouldn't even be looking at—namely, my mother. However, I've also never successfully stopped him from doing anything he wanted. It would be like delivering an order to Genghis Khan and expecting to walk away with your head still attached to your body. It's not something anyone is willing to try. Not since he shot Gianni Rossetti in the head at point-blank range twenty-five years ago.

Regardless, I'm not going to stand aside and watch while he chews up and spits out a woman who can't even begin to handle him.

Or maybe she could.

There's something about Drew that keeps me staring at her for longer than I should, and it's not her fantastic, curvy ass or her high, perky tits, or that long blond hair.

Actually, maybe it is the hair. Blond isn't her color, no matter how hot as fuck she looks with it curling down her back. She should have dark hair. Brunette or black. She'd be like a sleek black cat, and there's nothing I'd like to do more than make her purr.

Jesus. Where the fuck did that come from? I'm as bad as the old man, letting my dick get hard thinking about an employee. *And even worse, I'm lying if I say it's the first time it's happened.*

"We don't think you'll honor a truce," Giancarlo Tyrol Rossetti Sr. says, and my attention snaps back to the meeting happening in front of me.

"Don't you fucking question—" Lorenzo Angelini, Dom's new fucking idiot second in command says. But when Dom raises a hand, Enzo shuts the hell up like a good little dog as a tense silence hangs over everyone while Dom digests the senior Rossetti's insult.

I'm not technically supposed to be in this room. I'm the only member of the Casso clan who has a clean record and doesn't get jacked with regularly by cops who are willing to test Dom's temper. But since the meeting is happening at my club, which is a completely legitimate business, I'm listening from a place of honor—at Dom's side.

It's no secret that he wants me to fight for the right to take his position as head of the family someday. He'd like nothing more than to pit me against Enzo, a thug who has no problem smashing knees and enforcing debts, but can also pull off a half-decent impression of being slick and civilized when he wants to.

But if I'm being honest, Enzo's a hell of a lot more like Dom than I'll ever be.

"You don't think *I'll* honor the truce, Rossetti? You had a hand in fucking up the spa where my goddamned daughter went to work every day. Do you remember that bloodbath? I almost *lost* my girl over that."

Rossetti pales under his ruddy complexion.

I stay silent and still, shocked that Dom actually claimed Eden as his daughter, my half sister, out loud. Now that she's married to a tattoo artist in New Orleans and far away from the city, he has to assume she's safe and out of Rossetti's reach.

"We didn't know. Thought she was just another bitch running numbers for you."

Dom shoots to his feet. "She's my fucking flesh and blood. Do you know what I do to people who touch my flesh and blood? No, you fucking don't, because they're never fucking found again."

I know who he's talking about now, Creighton Karas's uncle. I've known Creighton was my half brother since childhood, but he hasn't known about our connection for nearly as long. Which is why Creighton still won't speak to me.

It's a long story, but suffice it to say that he was my best friend for decades. I ran his businesses, all legit, for years. Until he found out where my loyalty lay—with Dom.

If I could go back and change it, I'd be hard-pressed to

follow Dom's orders. I didn't realize how fucking much I'd miss being able to call my best friend and ask for advice. Not that I could ever talk to him about anything like this. He had no clue that I was planted in his boarding school to become his friend and keep tabs on him for our father. *None.* Until I leaked the wrong piece of information to Dom and there was no other person to take the fall. Then it all came out and I was banished from the Karas kingdom, and I slunk back to the gutter, a failure.

Dom hasn't let me live that down yet either. He still thinks that dangling the carrot of leadership of the family will make me do tricks for him, but I don't even know if I want it.

One thing is for certain, though—Enzo can't have it. The streets would run red with the blood of innocents, because he's a fucking psychopath.

Giancarlo leans back in his chair, puffing on his three-thousand-dollar cigar that the club won't be paid for. "You have my sincere apologies for my mistake, Casso. We'll accept the truce. But if something goes down and your fingerprints are on it, we will burn your family to the ground."

Beside him, GTR, his son, smirks. At least, he smirks until Dom rises and presses both palms on the table to stare them both down.

"Save your threats, Rossetti. If I find out that you're fucking us over, every last one of you will be dead. We understand each other?"

Giancarlo presses down on the arms of his chair to rise. He stares Dom down, eye to eye, as GTR shoves his chair back.

"We understand each other, Casso."

"Good. Then we have a deal." Dom extends his arm and

the two men shake hands, sealing the first truce between the families in a quarter of a century.

Dom speaks to me without breaking eye contact with the man across the table from him. "Cannon, get a box of those cigars Giancarlo likes. As a gesture of goodwill."

Goddamned motherfucker. Now I'll have to take over a $30,000 loss on this month's balance sheet, all because Rossetti likes Arturo Fuente Opus Xs and Dom wants to be generous.

I button my suit jacket as I stand. "Of course. I'll meet you at the door with them."

When I slip out of the conclave, Tanya comes toward me.

"Can I help with anything, Boss? More drinks? Cigars?"

"No. Meeting's over." Which reminds me that I didn't bring up in the meeting that Donny had recently shown up here. But with the truce . . . it means he can't step out of line now.

My gaze zeroes in on Drew where she hovers near the bar, as if clinging to Stefano's presence like a life preserver. *Smart girl.* I only have a second to make a decision, and I know what I need to do.

"Take Drew to the employee break room and show her out through the back entrance. Get her a car home. No one sees her," I say, never breaking eye contact with Drew.

My new waitress blinks twice and her brown eyes widen. At ten feet away, she can hear me plain as day. I swear I catch a glimpse of color that's not brown, but I'm too fucking riled up to know if I'm right or not.

"What?" Drew asks as Tanya goes rigid.

"You heard me. Go. Now."

Tanya wastes no time rushing over to Drew, grabbing her by the arm, and hurrying her out of the main room just before the conclave door opens. Dom comes out and immediately scans the club, looking for Drew just like I knew he would.

I stride to the glass-enclosed room where the inventory is kept and unlock the door. As soon as I've retrieved the box of cigars, I turn around to leave with them in hand, and Dom meets me at the door.

"Where is she?"

"Who?" My question is total bullshit, and we both know it.

"I want to see you in my office. Tomorrow. Noon. We have things to discuss. Be discreet." My father shoves his hands in his suit pants pockets and jangles the two coins he always carries. A reminder of how far he has risen since the days when he didn't have two nickels to rub together.

"I know the drill," I tell him from between clenched teeth.

"Good." He glances at the box of cigars in my hand. "Bring me a box of those too."

Fucking asshole. He doesn't even like this brand, but he wants to make it harder for me to have the club show a profit. It keeps me under his thumb.

Welcome to the world of being an illegitimate Casso. It's a fucking blast.

DREW

*T*anya's grip on my upper arm is tight enough to leave bruises as she drags me into the break room and presses a wooden panel that swings in to reveal another hidden door.

"What's going on?" I jerk out of her hold and spin around to face her.

"Grab your purse and don't ask any more stupid fucking questions."

I fumble for the key to my locker, yank out my purse and folded clothes, and follow her through the secret exit. As soon as the panel slides back into place, lights glow just brightly enough for me to see the gray industrial carpet beneath my feet.

"This bolt-hole leads to Cannon's private elevator, which is hidden from pretty much everyone." She flashes a key. "Only trusted employees can access it, and we only use it when he tells us to, or if some really bad shit goes down. Like right now. Come on."

She leads me to a set of stainless-steel doors and inserts the key to engage the elevator call button. As soon as the light is on, indicating the car is moving our way, she pulls out her phone and taps in a message. When she's finished, we slip inside and she punches *G*, I assume for garage.

"I don't know what the fuck you did, but I knew you wouldn't last long in this job. I just didn't realize how right I'd be."

"I didn't do anything besides the things you trained me to do," I tell her, crossing my arms.

Her blue eyes slice through me. "Bullshit. Because I wouldn't be hustling you out to a car with an armed driver at one in the morning if everything was fine."

I think of what Dominic Casso said. "Is it because . . . because of Dom?"

If I thought Tanya's gaze was cold before, now it's ice. "Don't talk about him. Don't even say his name." Her reaction is so much like Randi's that chill bumps prickle all over my skin.

"What am I supposed to do then?"

"Serve drinks and try to be invisible, if that's even a possibility now. Cannon's the only one who can clean up the mess you've made, and even then, it's dicey. Once *he* sees something he wants, there's pretty much nothing that can stop him from getting it."

She checks her phone again before shaking her head.

There's no question *he* is the one we're not supposed to talk about.

"I'm not interested in old men. Isn't it that easy?" I'm partly being honest and partly playing a role that says I don't know who Dominic Casso is and how dangerous he can be.

"You're a fucking idiot." Tanya shakes her head, making her light brown hair spill around her shoulders. "I didn't think it was possible for someone to be this dumb."

The elevator stops, and she tenses as the doors open. The garage is empty, but for the scent of exhaust, oil, and rubber.

"He should be here any minute. Probably got caught at a light," she says as she glances from side to side.

"Who?" I ask her, and this time the question is genuine.

"Your ride home. He'll walk you up to the door and make sure you get inside okay. Cannon does it for us whenever we need it, so don't feel special or anything."

Even though her comment is meant as a slap, I can't help but feel a warm pang in my chest that he makes sure his employees are safe. That is, *if* I'm still an employee after tonight.

"I didn't try to do anything—"

Tanya cuts off my protests. "You don't have to *try*. That's your problem. You're just like Teal. Men see you, and then they're tripping over their dicks to smell your hair and asking if they can buy you things."

I jerk my head back at the scowl on her face. More than anything, I feel like she just opened a window for me to learn more information that could possibly be helpful to piece together what the hell is going on here.

"Who's Teal?"

Tanya coughs, or maybe she's choking? "Like you don't know."

"I don't have any idea," I tell her as a black Escalade pulls up.

"Whatever. Get in the car. Wait for a text in the morning before you come in. Cannon might want you to take the day off to let things cool down, if he doesn't fire you. Try to stay out of trouble. Actually, don't even leave your apartment. It's safer."

Something in her voice transcends the catty, bitchy attitude, and I think it's concern.

"Ms. Tanya, it's a pleasure to see you," the driver of the SUV says as he slides out of the driver's seat and opens the back door.

"Likewise, Warren. Take care of her. Boss's orders."

"I always do."

"Thanks."

Tanya turns to walk away, but I reach out to grab her wrist.

"Hey. Whatever I did, I didn't mean to. Thanks for helping me."

She stares down at my hand on her arm and slowly drags her gaze to mine. "We're not friends. I don't like you, and don't ever touch me. Got it?"

I drop my hand and sigh. "Thanks again, Tanya. You're as delightful as ever."

* * *

ONCE SAFELY INSIDE MY APARTMENT, I lock it up tight with the dead bolt, secondary bolt, and chain before setting the security system.

My undercover persona wouldn't have the cash to live somewhere with a doorman, so I'm left hoping that I'll be secure enough with the measures I've put in place—a small wireless camera hidden in the entryway so I can see everyone who's coming and going, as well as one in the elevator lobby and another outside my door. Despite what Cannon and Tanya think of me, I'm not stupid. Not even close.

But tonight . . . *fuck*. I have no idea what happened. The last thing I wanted to do was attract Dominic Casso's attention like this. His interest could jeopardize my entire investigation, and I won't give up until justice is served and every single person who had a hand in my father's death is behind bars.

With a deep, calming breath, I center myself and consider the situation rationally.

Is there any way I can turn this to my advantage?

I can't be what Dom wants me to be. I'm not looking for a sugar daddy of any kind, let alone one who would have a detrimental impact on me still breathing after this is all over.

And the look on Cannon's face? Lord, I don't know if I'll ever forget that either. He was furious, but underlying it all was concern for my safety . . . and maybe something else. *Jealousy?*

No. I have to be imagining that. If he's with Tanya, there's no way he gives a damn about me, other than he probably doesn't want to have to hire someone new and start all over again.

But why do I like the idea of him being concerned about me for other reasons?

It's a dumb thought, so I shut it out of my head. I don't even like him. Hell, if he had something to do with my father's death, then I'll smile as they lead him off in shackles.

I wander through my apartment, barely noticing the blank white walls, bare of any pictures or anything personal that could possibly reveal my identity.

What the hell should I do now?

Tanya said not to come into work tomorrow without getting a text telling me it's okay. But what if it doesn't come? Normally, I have a plan B, C, D, E, and so on. But in this scenario, a completely unsanctioned investigation, I've only got my wits to lead me down the right path. And that path is *not* leading me to Dom Casso's bed.

A shudder racks my body, and this one I don't have to hide.

Wanting to forget all about tonight, I head for my counter, grab a bottle of red and a wineglass, and stroll toward the bathroom.

Bubble baths may not heal all wounds, but they're where I do some of my best thinking. And right now, everything is on the line.

13

CANNON

*D*ominic Casso could have upgraded from the brownstone at the edge of Hell's Kitchen decades ago if he'd wanted, but he elected to stay in the same place he's held court from the beginning of his reign. A sentimental man would assume it's because he wanted to stay close to his roots, but a sentimental man wouldn't last long in the Casso organization.

No, Dom chooses to stay here because he's a creature of habit in all the ways that won't get him killed. Not that there has been anyone with big enough balls to attempt that in the last twenty years. Still, for purely selfish reasons, I wish he'd sold this brownstone.

As I cross the street to walk up the steps to the entrance, a scene flashes vividly in my mind—the body of my mother, bleeding out from three gunshot wounds to the chest on these very steps.

That was the day I became just another kid dangling off the bastard branch of the Casso family tree. No family was eager to take me in, and I had a negligent father who only summoned me to his desk when he needed something.

Shortly after my mother was buried in a cemetery on Staten Island and my aunt was fretting over what would become of me, Dom sent a car to get me, and it dropped me off right here.

The scene of the crime.

To this day, I've never figured out if it was a test. Maybe he thought they'd bring a sniveling brat crying for his mommy up to the boss, and he could wash his hands of me for life with the ease of his signature across the bottom of a check for my upkeep. For the right price, my aunt would have been willing to make me her problem until I was eighteen. But that's not what I did.

My mother taught me from a young age that life wasn't kind to people like us. We existed on the goodwill of others, and it would behoove me to learn as much as I could as fast as I could, with the hopes that I'd be useful to someone higher up the food chain. I listened, studied hard, and watched everything around me, constantly wondering what scraps the world would throw my way.

It came that hot-as-hell summer morning, when Dom told me what my new role in life would be.

"You're going to boarding school, and not because I think you need that kind of fancy education, but because you're going to find a kid named Creighton Karas. He's the same age as you. Make yourself indispensable to him. Become his best friend. Keep tabs on him. Make sure nothing happens to him. And whatever he does, make sure you're a part of it. Then you're gonna report every goddamned thing back to me. Understand?"

I didn't understand, but I nodded anyway. That's all he needed from me before he sent me home to pack my stuff, carrying an envelope of cash for my aunt.

I've spent the rest of my life knowing I was sold to the mob for $2,500.

Twenty-five hundred dollars, and I never saw my aunt again, but my mother's words never faded. I made myself useful. Creighton Karas became my best friend. It wasn't too long before I realized he was my brother. I reported every goddamned move he made back to Dom.

Which subjects he excelled in—all of them.

Which teachers he didn't like—all of them.

Which girls tried to sneak into our room—all of them.

Every time I made my report, Dom would say the same thing. *"Good. Call me again next week. Stay out of trouble, kid."*

Never once did he ask me about my grades, my life at school, or anything personal. The whole time, I asked myself why the fuck he cared so goddamned much about Creighton and nothing about me. Even Cav and Eden got relatively better, and slightly less negligent, treatment.

I've always been the expendable one. The least in favor. And I always told myself I didn't give a fuck, because Dominic Casso's opinion of me would never affect the man I became. Who I am, everything I've done, is in spite of him, not because of him.

When I fell out of favor with Creighton, a large part of me assumed that was it. Dom would finally take me out with the trash where he's made it so apparent I belong. It hasn't happened yet, but that's not to say it couldn't happen anytime.

So, why do I keep working for him? Because at the end of the day, I can't shake the need to prove myself. It's fucking pathetic, but it's the truth.

As soon as I grip the ornate brass handle of the building— too nice twenty years ago, but it perfectly fits in with the gentrification that has swept the area since—Primo nods at me from inside the entrance.

"Boss said you were coming. Figured you'd be early, like

usual," the big man says with his hand resting casually on the gun tucked beneath his suit jacket. He's a carbon copy of his brother Tempo, one of Dom's other trusted bodyguards.

"How's it going, man? Did you catch the replay of the Mets game? Hell of a seventh inning." I make small talk with the guys, not because I give a shit about baseball, but because it's expected.

"Nah, Boss didn't head home until after three, so I didn't catch shit. But I'll make sure to check SportsCenter after I'm off. Head on up, Mr. Freeman. I'm sure he knows you're here."

I punch the call button for the elevator.

You'd think we'd have a few more minutes to shoot the shit because the equipment would be slow as hell in a building like this, but Dom replaced the elevators in every building he owned with high-end models a few years ago, when things started to get bloody again with the Rossettis. Only the most trusted of Dom's people know about the hidden elevators that offer a second escape route in each building.

Once in the car, I'm taken straight up to the top, and Pietro is waiting to give me a chin lift as I step out.

"Nice to see you, Mr. Freeman. He should be ready for you."

"Thanks."

Pietro, Primo, Tempo, and Umberto are Dom's equivalent of the Secret Service. They might look big and slow, but they're actually smarter than you'd guess. They're Italian boys who played football and graduated from college, courtesy of the same scholarship I got—Dom Casso's checkbook.

One thing is absolutely certain, though; their loyalty is to the death, and two of the four have already taken bullets for him. One of them is always with Dom, and there's always someone watching the brownstone despite its crazy security setup.

Pietro opens the door that leads to hell's waiting room, or at least that's what I've always called it. Because inside, your life always hangs in the balance, and I'm pretty sure every man who hasn't made it out alive had a one-way ticket to dance with the devil.

A woman in her sixties with perfectly coifed gray hair and a brown-and-pink dress sits at the desk outside the unadorned wood door that leads to Dom's office. With her glasses hanging around her neck on a beaded chain, she's always reminded me of a librarian who wouldn't hesitate to shush you if you got too rowdy. But behind that grandmotherly exterior is the heart of a warrior and the tenacity of a bulldog. I've watched her pull a gun and use it, to protect herself and her boss.

"Marta. You're looking as lovely as ever."

Her cheeks turn rosier as I stride toward her. "Mr. Freeman. It's a pleasure to see you, as always."

"How are the grandkids?"

"Getting so big. I wish they came with a pause button so I could enjoy it more before they turn into mouthy little brats who I'll have to threaten with visits from the boss."

I've always liked Marta, and I've often wondered if in her younger years she was one of Dom's original mistresses. Highly unlikely, given the fact that she's had gray hair and has worked for him for as long as I can remember, but you never know around here. In the Casso organization, it's not whether you've got skeletons in your closet, but how well you hid them to avoid being haunted.

I'm doing just fine with mine, but that could change at any moment. Dominic Casso likes to keep us all on our toes.

As soon as I step inside, my footsteps muffled by the

thickly padded green carpet that's regularly replaced due to stubborn bloodstains, I'm greeted with the sight of Dom flipping through an account book at his desk. Light pours in through the bulletproof glass that I'm still surprised he hasn't bricked over, because he's always worried someone's going to take him out in his own home. When he looks up, his steel-gray hair stays put in its exact style. It's been holding on stubbornly for years, as if it's scared to do him the indignity of falling out and leaving him bald.

"Good afternoon, sir."

When I speak, he slaps the book shut and looks up.

"Always early," he says in lieu of a greeting I wasn't expecting anyway. His dark gaze, nearly black, sweeps over me. "You'd think I wouldn't start wondering what the fuck is going on until you started rolling up late, but no. I'm wondering what the fuck is going on, because you're getting in my way."

Dom doesn't invite me to sit, which he never does, so I stand between the door and the worn brown leather guest chairs. Staying on my feet makes it easier to dodge flying objects and bullets, which aren't out of the realm of possibility, because I know exactly what he wants to talk about today.

"I didn't intend to get in your way, sir. Can you clarify?"

His gaze narrows as he plants his elbows on the surface of the large desk. "You can't bullshit a bullshitter. Don't pretend you don't know what I'm talking about. The girl."

If respect for this old, yet deadly man hadn't been practically beaten into me for over thirty years, I probably would have turned around and walked out, or even said something like *she's too young for you and your Viagra prescription*. But I'm not ready for my body to be found floating in the East River quite yet.

"Which girl?"

"The only one you made sure I couldn't see last night after the meeting. I don't know what the fuck you did with her, but I want her." Dom shoves the account book aside as his nostrils flare.

Fuck, he's pissed. Normally, I wouldn't think of sticking my nose where it doesn't belong, especially in Dom's personal business, but I can't let this happen.

Drew Carson isn't the kind of woman who could survive being Dom's mistress. I may not know her well, but I know that much.

I don't even acknowledge the scalding pit of jealousy that brews in my gut at the thought of him putting his hands on her. I already saw how he watched her. Knowing this was coming, I try the nonchalant tactic first.

"Do you know how hard it is to find good help? If you want the club to keep running the way it has been, and the cash to keep flowing, you'll find someone else. She's got potential, and I can't afford to lose her."

Dom steeples his fingers and spears me with those satanically black eyes. "I don't give a fuck. You can find someone else. Someone better. Hell, raise the wages. I'll approve it."

"Why her?" I ask, keeping my tone as disinterested as possible.

"I like the way she laughs."

The vat of jealousy boils over and his comment stings me. *He likes the way she laughs?* I've never fucking heard her laugh, and now it seems like a massive oversight. I may regret what I'm about to say, but I don't know how else to handle the situation. So I lie.

"With all due respect, sir, you're too late. Drew Carson is off-limits."

Dom's glare sharpens. "What the fuck did you say to me, kid?"

I stalk to the guest chair and grip the back, not allowing myself to shrink in front of the man who wants me to roll over for him. Not this time. "She's off-limits. You're going to have to find someone else to laugh for you."

Shoving his elbows off the desk, Dom leans back in his chair, his dark gaze drilling into me. "No one's off-limits to me. You know that."

"First time for everything."

As the statement he doesn't want to hear comes out of my mouth, Dom's already ruddy cheeks turn brighter red and his fingers flex tighter. "Who's her man? I'll take care of him. Not a fucking problem."

Static crackles in my ears, and the thrum of my pulse slows until I'm cold and controlled. Then I drop the equivalent of the A-bomb. The only thing that'll win this war.

"Me. I'm her man."

14

CANNON

*D*om's head jerks back, and he stares at me in shock. "*You*? No fucking way. The original *all work, no play* boy."

He pauses, and laughter spills from his previously flattened lips.

"No *playboy* either. So, tell me what the fuck you're trying to pull here, because I don't believe this shit. You think she's too young for me? You think I can't get it up for a grade A piece of ass like that anymore? Is that what you think, Cannon?"

Anyone else might get riled up to have shit like that thrown at them, but I've got a lifetime of practice in keeping my cool. What I'm not used to is lying to Dom about something like this. Good thing I honed all my skills on his dime at fancy boarding schools and an Ivy League college.

"I don't give a shit how your dick's working, Dom. It's not going anywhere near her. I saw her first. I staked my claim. There are millions of other women in this city who would be more than happy to oblige you. But Drew Carson is *mine*." I shove the heavy chair toward his desk and push off it.

Dom leans back in his chair, his arms crossed over his chest, and a strange light enters his eyes. Flickering. Flashing. Scheming.

"You haven't had a permanent bitch in years, so why her? Why now? Afraid your cock'll fall off from lack of regular use?"

"You saw her. Is it shocking to think I saw her and wanted to fuck her?" As soon as the words are out, I realize they're the honest fucking truth. I do want her. I've wanted her from the first second I saw her. Saying it out loud just gives it more power.

"You're fucking already?" He tilts his head to the side in a move that tells me there's no way he'll believe me if I say yes. Basically, he's waiting to catch me in a lie, but I'm smarter than that.

"I'm working on it."

Dom purses his lips in a move that makes him look like a teenage girl trying to make duck lips for a selfie, and I know what that means. Nothing good.

"Then far be it from me to try to cock-block my own . . . man."

When he trailed off, it sounded like he was about to say *son* and then changed his mind. Dom has gone this long without ever officially acknowledging me, so I'm not surprised by how he finished the sentence.

But right now, I've got more important things to think about than my paternity. A rush of victorious relief shoots through me, but I don't let it show in my expression or posture.

I should have known that it was too much triumph, too soon.

"Matter of fact," Dom says, a cruel smile curling his lips. "How about I help you out with her?"

I clench my teeth together to keep from speaking until I hear what he has to say.

"You can have my table tonight at Per Se. Eight o'clock. She deserves something nice."

Motherfucker. From that damned gleam in his eye, it's clear he thinks he's won. That he's going to get me to fuck this up, and he'll sweep in and snatch her away from me, and the lies I've told won't help her any.

Not on my watch.

"Thanks. I appreciate that, Dom. Glad you don't mind I'll be taking the entire night off." I keep my tone casual, but there's a wholly separate silent conversation happening between our locked stares.

"You can't fool me, boy. You're full of shit, and I'll have men watching the restaurant to report back when you don't show."

"I'll be there, old man. And I'll spend the rest of the night with her, so you'll have no question that she's mine."

I end the stare-down by shoving my hands in my suit pants pockets. "Is there anything else you need before I head to the club? I've got a lot of work to do before dinner."

One side of Dom's mouth curls up in a sneer as his eyes turn hooded. "Not unless you've managed to bridge the gap with Creighton after you fucked that up."

He'll take any opportunity to twist the knife about the brother I lost because I wasn't willing to lie to him anymore, even though Dom doesn't need me to shadow Creighton and report back. The old man talks to him regularly. Even attended the fucking baptism for Rose that I barged in on in an effort to warn Creighton that having Dom anywhere near his daughter was a horrible mistake. My interference didn't go over well. At all.

"No, sir."

"Then, nah. Get the fuck out." He uncrosses his arms to

wave me off, but I'm already heading for the door and fresh air not weighed down by disappointment and disgust.

When I finally hit the sidewalk, I take a breath and consider what the hell I've done.

How the fuck am I going to get Drew to agree?

"*C*annon wants to see you in his office," Tanya says as she sweeps into the kitchen where I'm plating salads for a group of Wall Street bankers having a late three-martini lunch after the closing bell.

My victory of the day, after getting the text from Cannon that it was all clear for me to come into work, was convincing the bankers to buy a thirty-thousand-dollar box of cigars for the table to split.

"About what?" I glance over my shoulder at her as she fills a cup with lobster bisque and sets it on a gold-and-white china saucer. My nerves have been going haywire all day because of the *mob boss hitting on me* episode last night.

"He didn't say." She replaces the ladle and fits the lid on the tureen before shooting me a smug smile. "But I'm sure it won't take long. He said something about you needing to leave early."

Fuck. No. He can't fire me. He can't. I'm not any closer to finding answers than I was before I started working here. Other than the fact that Cannon Freeman is a contradiction I can't begin to unravel or explain. *I need more time.*

She stops next to me, checking over the salads I've painstakingly assembled, and smirks. "I'll finish those. Doesn't sound like you'll have time."

With a steadying breath, I stop myself from flinging micro greens in her face. "Thanks. I appreciate your help, Tanya."

The triumphant twinkle in her eyes brightens. "Don't mention it."

Taking one measured step at a time, I exit the kitchen and cross the floor, smiling at the club members whose gazes I catch as I approach the hidden panel.

Once I'm inside, the muted chatter on the club floor silences. Only twenty feet of red-and-gold carpet and richly stained walls separate me from the potential first roadblock in my journey for justice—Cannon Freeman.

"I'm not going to let him take this from me," I whisper quietly so that the cameras and microphones that cover every inch of this place can't pick up my words.

When I reach the door, I knock.

"Enter," he calls.

I twist open the handle and step inside to be greeted by the library-esque scent of books. No matter how long I live, I'll forever associate that fragrance with the dark-haired man sitting at the desk in front of me.

When he looks up, my palms are already sweating, which is ridiculous because I've been embedded with troops checking the roadside for IEDs. This shouldn't even cause a blip in my blood pressure. But it does, because never before has any investigation been so personal. Which is probably why Ariel told me to leave it alone and pay someone else to dig into it for me. But I'm convinced no one else could handle this like I could, and I still am.

Which is why I blurt out words I don't intend to say.

"Please don't fire me. It wasn't intentional."

Cannon's glittering hazel eyes lift to rake over my face. "Who said I was firing you?"

"Umm. No one, exactly, but . . ." I pause, not wanting to throw Tanya under the bus due to some misplaced sense of loyalty I didn't know I felt. "I was under the impression you didn't need me to stay until the end of my shift, and the only reason I could think of to explain that was because I wouldn't be employed here any longer."

My explanation comes out stiffer than one would expect from someone who used to broadcast hard-hitting news reports to millions of people.

Cannon tosses the pen onto his blotter and opens a drawer. "You're not fired, but you are leaving." He tosses a card onto my side of the desk and waves at me to take it.

I reach down to pick up the thick red card stock, which is stamped with a name everyone in New York knows, but I'm confused by why he's offering it to me.

BARNEYS
NEW YORK

"GO TO BARNEYS. Sally and Britta are expecting you. I'll pick you up at seven forty-five from the salon entrance."

I stare at Cannon like he's just told me I'm going on a quick drug run across the border. "Excuse me?"

"Barneys. Dress. Hair. Makeup. They'll all be covered on my account."

A chant starts in my head. *Oh, my wig, I'm so fucked. Oh, my wig, I'm so fucked.*

"But . . . but . . . why?"

Cannon's hazel eyes lock onto mine. "Because we're going on a date to save you from becoming Dom Casso's next mistress."

* * *

I WALK OUT of the break room clutching my purse. A moment ago, if you'd asked me to describe the expression I saw in the mirror on the inner panel of my locker, it would have been shell-shocked. *How can I possibly keep this from happening without raising red flags?*

When I step onto the floor of the club, Tanya zips to my side like she's been waiting for me to appear.

"It was nice knowing you. If you forgot anything in your locker, we'll mail it to you."

"She'll be back tomorrow, Tanya." Cannon's deep voice comes from behind me.

How the hell does he move so quietly? He's like a lone wolf, silently stalking his prey.

While I shut down the overactive part of my imagination, Tanya sputters.

"Wh-what? Oh. Sorry. I thought . . ."

"Call Teal. Tell her there's a driver coming to get her. I don't care where she is or what she's doing, she's making her damn shift and she'd better be sober."

With the first sheepish look I've seen on her face, Tanya slinks in the direction from which I just came.

Who is Teal, and why are we worried she won't be sober?

My neck prickles as Cannon comes closer to me, and I slowly turn to face him.

"Now I understand why you thought you were getting fired. I'll talk to her about giving you shit."

"No. Don't," I say quickly, wanting to cut that idea off as quickly as it came to life, especially since he told me to deal with her on my own, which I've been doing just fine. "It'll just make it worse. I can handle her."

His gaze sweeps over my face. "I don't doubt that. Now get the hell out of here. Your car is waiting out front."

16

DREW

*G*etting the hell out of the club is absolutely no problem for me, but the car waiting for me on the street is. I can't dodge Warren because the Escalade is double-parked, and he opens the back door as soon as he sees me step onto the sidewalk.

"Ms. Carson, it's a pleasure."

"Hi, Warren," I say with a tight smile, my brain still battling over my fight-or-flight decision.

Pedestrians dodge around where my heels are glued to the concrete. In one direction is Barneys, where I face possible discovery. In the other direction is my apartment, where I can hide and pretend this isn't happening, but then I risk being claimed as the mistress of a man I'm only here to put in prison.

Stay cool. Act cool. Be cool. I glance up at the sky and take a few seconds to just breathe. And yet, no solutions magically appear.

Really, universe? Is this how you want me to play it?

Clearly, there's no reply. At least, not until someone slams into my shoulder.

"You're blocking the sidewalk. Get the hell out of the—" Before the man finishes speaking, Warren is between us.

"Don't say another word to the lady, or you'll regret it."

The man in a suit glares at Warren for a half second before Warren's jacket flaps open to reveal a gun. The man's eyes widen, and he backs away. "Whoa, man. Sorry."

"Move the fuck on," Warren says in a low tone, and then leads me to the SUV. "Sorry about that, Ms. Carson. It won't happen again. I'll escort you from the door. Mr. Freeman would have my ass if I didn't make sure you arrive safe and sound."

And that's how I find myself settled in the back of a Cadillac, heading for Barneys. It reminds me of how my father would tell me, *"Not making a decision is the same as making one. You've always got a choice, even when it's refusing to choose."*

Sadness scores my chest, and I fight the mist of tears coming over my eyes. It's been almost eight months, but from the sharpness of the pain, it still feels like yesterday.

They say time heals all wounds, but that's bullshit. Nothing will ever heal this wound. Justice is the next best thing. Which means if I have to go on one date with Cannon Freeman to save my investigation, so be it.

Warren slides into the driver's seat and pulls into traffic. It takes us twenty minutes to get to Barneys. He helps me out of the car and tells me he and Mr. Freeman will pick me up in the same spot at 7:45.

With a smile, I head inside the flagship department store, ready to face my next test, and a high-pitched voice squeaks, "Lizzy? Is that you?"

Oh. Fuck.

Thankfully, it's been a long time since I've answered to the name Lizzy, so I don't acknowledge the hesitant question. I keep walking forward until the woman, a contact I used for an investigation four years ago, rushes up to me. Mindy Vick. That's her name.

But as soon as she sees my face, she jerks back.

"Oh, sorry. I thought you were someone else. My bad. Have a good one."

I smile and nod, not trusting my voice right now, because the moment she called me *Lizzy*, my British accent bubbled up in my throat, just like every time I used that alias.

With perfect timing, a dark-haired woman sweeps up to my side, and Mindy scurries out of earshot.

"Ms. Carson?"

I meet her clear gray gaze and force the British accent down. "Are you Sally or Britta?"

"Yes, I'm Britta. It's a pleasure to meet you. I understand you need a dress for dinner at Per Se."

I can only imagine what Cannon told her, but from the way she's sizing me up, I have a feeling I'm not what she expected. This isn't a *Richard Gere sends Julia Roberts to Rodeo Drive because she has no decent dress* situation, and for some reason, I get the sense that's the scene she was expecting to play out.

I shine my brightest smile on her as I shake my head in what I hope is an indulgent fashion. "He really does go overboard with wanting to spoil me sometimes."

I don't know why I make it sound like this is a normal occurrence for Cannon and me, but I'm following my instincts here. Something tells me Britta might want Cannon for herself. *Or maybe she already had him.* I brush the thought away as Britta's smile falters.

"How lucky for you. Why don't you come with me? I have a selection already pulled based on his comments, but now I'm wondering if you wouldn't rather just pick your own."

Yep, she was totally expecting Pretty Woman. Maybe even hoping for it?

I follow her trim figure, graceful in her Manhattan uniform of all black, toward the area where the couture gowns and dresses are displayed. "Simple and elegant. That's all I need."

It's on the tip of my tongue to tell her I don't want to put it on his account either, because I have my own, but that would be the height of stupidity. *It won't be weird to wear something he paid for. Consider it a costume,* I tell myself, but even I know that's not true.

There's something very alpha and dominant about a man clothing a woman, and therefore, I shall pretend it doesn't affect me. *And here I am, lying to myself.*

In the lavish private dressing area, meant for personal shoppers and their clients, she shows me an array of dresses. Five of the six are ugly as sin. High fashion, expensive as hell, and proof once more that it doesn't matter what label and price tag you put on things, some are just freaking hideous.

The last is a simple black A-line cocktail dress with a low-cut bodice and almost no ornamentation.

"If you don't like any of these, I'm happy to bring in a selection more to your taste."

I shake my head. "I'll try the black one. I need a size—"

"Mr. Freeman provided your dress size. I just need your shoe size, and I can pull some heels for you to try on with it."

"Eight," I murmur, and she hands me the dress and disappears in search of shoes.

How the hell did he know what size I wear? A wave of heat washes over me as I close the door to the private dressing room and stare down at the tag. He was absolutely right about the size, though. *Is he really watching me that closely?*

As I slip out of my uniform, I'm utterly aware of the slide

of fabric across my skin. It's almost as if I can feel him watching me right now. Another unwelcome punch of arousal slams into me.

I am not attracted to him. I can't be. This isn't a real date. It's a fact-finding mission. An interview. That's it. That's all.

But as soon as I have the black dress on, I can't help but picture him taking it off of me.

Dammit.

I close my eyes, but I can't get the vision out of my mind. Cannon's wide, capable hands sliding the cap sleeves off my shoulders and letting the bodice slip over my bare skin.

Shit. Stop. No.

I flick open my eyes to bring me back to reality, because the liquid feeling low in my belly means nothing good for me and my investigation.

Giving the mirror one last quick glance, I can't get out of the damn dressing room fast enough.

WITH MY DRESS bag in hand, now containing my work clothes while I wear the gorgeous black number and the heels Britta selected, the personal shopper escorts me to the salon. Sally, the revered owner, crosses the floor to greet us.

As soon as Britta leaves, Sally tilts her head to the side and studies me. Before she speaks, I know she knows my secret.

"You're wearing a wig. I wasn't told to expect that. Why? What are we working with here?"

Activity buzzes in the salon, and I lower my voice to whisper my rehearsed lie so only Sally can hear me. "He's into blondes . . . but my hair is dark, and I love it too much to kill it with peroxide and bleach. But after tonight, I don't think he'll give a damn what color my hair is, if you know what I mean." I add a little wink for effect, hoping I'm not overplaying my hand.

For a moment, Sally's face stays stony. Then she throws her head back and laughs so loudly that every woman in the salon pauses to look at her. When she finishes cackling and chuckling, she smiles widely at me.

"You are a smart woman. I like you. He will never know—until it's too late."

A shiver of foreboding skates down my spine, and it almost feels like Sally's making a prediction that applies to a hell of a lot more than hair.

"Thank you. I appreciate your discretion, ma'am."

With a gleam in her faded blue eyes, she leads me to a station in the front. "Call me Sally. We women have to stick together. When I'm done, no man will be able to resist you. The rest is up to you."

An hour and a half later, I look freaking phenomenal. The simple dress sets off my expertly curled and arranged hair—and Sally refitted the wig even better than I could so that it's secure and perfect. The makeup artist followed my touch-up instructions to the letter, perfecting my contour, since Drew's cheekbones are much sharper than mine are normally.

I could tell she wanted to ask why I was wearing ten pounds of makeup, but she was polite enough not to voice the question.

Sally, who bonded with me over sisterhood and shared stories of the lovers in her past, gave me one final piece of advice before I left the salon.

"You're like me, self-possessed and sure. Don't be afraid of a little uncertainty in your life now and then. Sometimes it's exactly what you need to flourish."

Her words follow me out to the sidewalk, where, at 7:44, a Bentley pulls up at the curb and Cannon climbs out of the back seat.

Oh no. Not. Fair. It should be illegal for a man to look that good in a suit.

He also changed, because he didn't have a tie on earlier. The one he's wearing now is a silvery gray with a green stripe that manages to match his eyes perfectly.

I wonder if Britta picked it out for him. Another unwarranted stab of jealousy accompanies the thought, and I bat it away.

Fact-finding mission. Interview. Not a date.

But even the reminder can't stop the throbbing between my legs. *Hell.*

17

CANNON

"C hrist," I murmur under my breath.

Drew walks out of the salon on stilettos I want digging into my back while I pound into her until she screams my name. This is not how tonight is supposed to go.

I'm *supposed* to have a platonic dinner with an employee I can't put my dick in. And then when the dinner is over, I'm *supposed* to give myself a pat on the back for keeping her out of Dom's clutches.

But the only thing I can think about right now, or with, is my dick. Blood rushes south, making the traitor twitch against the silk lining of my suit pants.

I want her.

Every possessive instinct that roared to the forefront when Dom tried to claim her comes rushing back tenfold.

This isn't in my plans. *But why not? Why can't I have her? Who the fuck can stop us if we're both interested?*

I grapple with my rules until she halts in front of me. *Fuck it. I'm going with my gut.*

"You look beautiful, Drew. Stunning."

Her makeup is so perfectly applied that it hides the blush

I imagine rising on her cheeks. I have the sudden urge to wipe it all off so I can just see *her*.

"Thank you." Her gaze sweeps down to the toes of my wing tips and back up to my tie. "You look quite dapper yourself."

The compliment feels forced, and I remember that she's in a position she didn't ask for. It's up to me to make this easier on both of us.

"Come on, our table will be ready when we get there." With one hand on the small of her back, I help her into the Bentley, and once the door is closed behind us, Warren returns to the driver's seat and pulls away from the curb.

Traffic is bumper to bumper this time of night getting from Madison to Fifth. But as we turn on Fifty-Ninth heading for Columbus Circle, the rest of the city fades away, and I'm acutely aware of the woman beside me.

"Britta and Sally took care of you?" It's a stupid question given how gorgeous she looks, and I have no idea why I'm making small talk when silence is my default setting.

"Very helpful. Sally was fabulous."

What's left unsaid is more telling. "Britta wasn't?"

Drew glances at me out of the corner of her eye. "She was . . . interesting. Do you often send women in for her to dress?"

The question is fair, but I'm reluctant to answer. She doesn't need to know I've never even considered doing something like that because I've never wanted to give someone the wrong impression.

My life isn't built for attachments. It's built for discretion. Anyone who becomes close to me automatically enters the potential line of fire, whether I want to admit it or not.

Dom may not have recognized me as his son, but it's the worst-kept secret in this town. There are plenty of people—

with the Rossettis being at the top of the list, and probably some in the Casso crew—who wouldn't hesitate to take me out if they could get away with it.

Drew turns her head toward me, and I'm only fucking human—a human who wants those ruby-slicked lips wrapped around my cock.

The answer comes out without my permission.

"No. Never. Only you."

Her eyebrows arch upward. "No wonder she was expecting a prostitute with a heart of gold who needed to be made over into a lady."

I choke on a laugh and cough. "What?"

"*Pretty Woman*. The movie. Never mind." Drew sits back in her seat and stares straight ahead.

"If she wasn't particularly friendly to you, that's because she's . . . well, she . . ." I don't normally stumble over words, but I can't figure out how to say it politely.

"She wants to go for a ride on a loaded cannon named Cannon?" Drew asks, catching me with a sideways glance that makes me want to drag her into my lap. Only iron-clad self-control stops me as she continues. "I get it. I'm not an idiot. You don't need to explain or worry that I'm offended. I know this is just because—"

I hold up a hand to stop her from saying what's going to come out of her mouth next as my arousal slams into a concrete wall. Warren is as loyal as I can expect him to be, but I'll never completely trust anyone not to spy on me and report back to Dom. After all, it would be cosmic poetic justice after what I did to Creighton.

Thankfully, Drew picks up on my gesture and goes silent. Her gaze flicks to Warren and then back at me.

"Because you want me to do the same," she says, finishing

the sentence in a completely different manner than I think she normally would have.

My mind goes right back to where it left off—how much I wish I could drag her over top of me and say *fuck dinner*. Hell, that would be just as effective, especially if Warren is informing on me. Instead, I steal another appreciative glance at Drew and then force my gaze straight out the windshield again.

Stop. Thinking. About. Fucking. Her.

But it's impossible. She's a beautiful woman, who's smart and private and doesn't want a damn thing to do with me. Apparently, that's the recipe for my downfall.

Who fucking knew?

18

DREW

*C*annon waves Warren off in favor of helping me out of the car himself. I know this is all a sham, but the heat of his hand burning through the fabric of my dress at the small of my back keeps making me forget the ruse.

The maître d' lights up as soon as we enter the heavy blue doors that mark the entrance.

"Mr. Freeman, it is a pleasure to serve you tonight. We have your table ready for you and your lovely companion."

With his hand on my back like it belongs there, Cannon nods at the man with a confident smile. "Thank you, Hugo. We appreciate it."

Hugo leads us through a maze of tables in the bright space, overlooking Central Park and the statue of Columbus, and indicates a perfectly set table in a private corner with a wave of his hand. "Here you are, sir. Madam."

After he pulls out my chair, Cannon thanks him, and Hugo backs away politely.

Now comes the awkward part. I'm staring at my boss and target across a table in a restaurant where people come to impress, celebrate, woo, seduce, and more.

The ambience in the restaurant is muted, but there's enough background noise that I hope it's safe to ask the question that's about to pop off my tongue, whether I want to ask it or not.

"Can you please explain why we're here?"

Cannon's full lower lip presses against the upper as he studies me. Finally, after a few seconds, he says, "I told you why."

I shake my head carefully so as not to move a single hair of my wig that Sally expertly styled. "No. Not really. You gave orders. And since I'm assuming you don't want to say a certain someone's name in public, let's talk about Frank, the person I literally bumped into on the sidewalk leaving my interview with you, whose attention I did nothing to attract."

Cannon leans back in his seat, his lips quirking, and I assume it's with amusement over me renaming Dom Casso *Frank.* "Wrong."

I blink at him like he's crazy and shake my head. "No. Not wrong. I didn't do anything. I swear to God. If you brought a bible, I would swear to it on that too."

"That's just it," Cannon says, the other corner of his mouth lifting. "You don't realize the effect you have on men. All men. You're like a damned magnet. They—*we*—can't keep our eyes off you."

Silently, I curse myself for not making *Drew* a little homelier. Just enough to be cute because of her awesome personality, but not enough to attract unwanted attention. But it's too late now. It would be really hard to explain if I showed up looking different tomorrow.

I release a sigh that's only halfhearted, because *Cannon just admitted he's drawn to me too.* Not that I should care. At all. Not one little bit. *But I do.*

I unfold my napkin and drop it on my lap, forcing my

attention back to the subject at hand before the heat blooming between my legs gets even more out of control.

"So, Cannon, are you going to tell me what your plan is to keep me out of Frank's clutches?"

19

CANNON

*S*omehow, I don't think Drew wants to hear the plan currently in my head, because right now it involves eating her for dinner and saying *fuck the rest of this charade*. Because it's no longer an act I'm putting on for Dom.

I want her for myself.

Maybe there's some truth to the old adage *like father, like son*.

She's vibrant and full of fire, yet mistrustful of me and everything I represent, which reaffirms her intelligence.

"So . . . I take it that's the *no, I don't have a plan* response?" Drew asks quietly to fill the silence, instead of waiting for me to gather words together and make a rational statement.

"The plan revolves around the concept of the lesser of two evils," I state simply as I snag my own napkin off my plate. "And taking a beautiful woman out to dinner is no hardship for me, even if I am out of practice."

Her eyebrows, several shades darker than her blond hair, shoot up. "You? Out of practice? I find that hard to believe."

I tilt my head to the side, wondering what kind of stories she's been told about me and who her informant was. There are certainly plenty of rumors that could be making the rounds, many of them true, but the vast majority are more urban legend than fact.

"I don't get out of the club much, and I don't want to talk about work, *Frank*, or other women. So, what do you say we just enjoy a nice dinner together?"

Her chin dips toward the table for a beat before lifting. "Like a real date?"

I nod in reply, and Drew's dark eyes cut to the window. Once again, I swear I see something lighter flash in them.

Is she wearing colored contacts?

Before I have a chance to ask, she says, "I don't really know how to be on a date. I've been pretty busy for the last few years. Not a lot of free time to just . . . be." Her gaze sweeps back to mine, and I forget my earlier thought because she looks so . . . *sad.*

"Why not?"

Her chest rises beneath the low-cut neckline of that simple but fucking sexy-as-hell black dress, and I force myself to look away from the curves of her breasts because I want to focus on her answer.

Her red lips press together before she speaks. "It's been a rough few months. Sometimes life just doesn't give you many breaks, so you make what you can of it."

"What happened?"

Drew shakes her head. "Nothing good. Let's talk about something else."

The sadness morphs her expression into one that grips my chest and squeezes. *Why do I care?* I shouldn't. *But I do.* Probably for the same reason that I couldn't let Dom come anywhere near her with ownership on his mind.

Fuck. She's going to get me in trouble.

It's an instinct I can't ignore. Still, even knowing that isn't enough to make me back off now. It's been a long damn time since I've wanted something for myself, and if Drew is willing, this is happening between us.

The server and sommelier appear to take our orders for water, wine, and our dining selection for the evening. As plate after plate of tiny portions of food come out, part of me expected Drew to awkwardly assess each course, trying to guess what it is, but she does the exact opposite. She eats with aplomb, using the proper utensils, and never misses a beat.

That's when I know for certain there's a hell of a lot Drew Carson is hiding. She's familiar with haute cuisine, including oysters with pearls, pâté, foie gras, and every other food I could easily avoid for the rest of my life.

When the veal medallions are served, she pushes her plate forward. "I'm going to pass on this course, if you don't mind. Feel free to eat mine too."

"You don't like veal?"

An awkward expression crosses her face, her cheeks pinching and eyes squinting. "That's not exactly it."

"Then what?"

"It's delicious. Seriously great. And I know that because I ate it by accident once without knowing what it was. But when I know . . . I just can't."

Immediately, I know what her hang-up is. "You feel bad about eating it."

She nods tightly, staring at her plate, and I have to believe that beneath her makeup, she's turning green around the gills.

"Let's get out of here."

Drew's face jerks up to meet my gaze. "Like right now?"

"Yeah. I already know I'm going to be fucking starving after we leave, and I'd much prefer to eat at the Halal Guys' cart than finish whatever else we have coming, if you want to know the truth." I wad up my napkin and toss it on the table beside my plate.

Drew releases a sigh that disappears into the clinking of silverware and china around us. "Oh, thank God, because I think I'm going to puke if I don't get away from this veal, and I really don't like foie gras. I've just trained myself to eat it without gagging."

2 0

DREW

*C*annon's shoulders shake as booming laughter spills from him in a full-body laugh. The kind that reminds me of how my father would take every opportunity for mirth, not caring how many people would turn and stare, even when we were out in public. Hell, even in church sometimes.

Cannon's the same. Totally oblivious to all the faces in the restaurant that have turned to stare at us as he rises, still chuckling.

There was literally no bad mood that my father's laughter couldn't bring me out of. It was a cure-all that I will never experience again. Tears spring up in my eyes and I try to blink them away, but Cannon's laughter silences as concern creases his brow.

"Hey, what's wrong?" he asks as he holds out a hand.

I close my eyes for a second and successfully tamp down the waterworks. "Your laugh reminds me of someone. Someone I lost." When I meet his gaze again, his fingers curl around the fist I didn't realize I was clenching.

"I'm so sorry. That wasn't my intention."

I shake my head, trying to play it off, but Cannon's serious expression tells me how badly I'm failing.

"It's fine. I just . . . I thought I'd never hear someone laugh like that again. It surprised me. I'm fine."

Carefully, Cannon helps me up from my chair, and we're standing a breath apart, in the middle of a restaurant with dozens of people looking at us.

This is no time to break down.

Injecting levity I don't feel into my voice, I ask, "How about that halal?" Except, as soon as I say it, the maître d' is at our table.

"Is something wrong, Mr. Freeman? Is the cuisine not to your liking? We can have something else prepared."

Mortification washes over me, and I'm thankful for my thick layers of makeup to hide my blush as Cannon responds.

"It was great. Put it on Dom's tab. Something else came up, and we've got to run."

Cannon places his hand on the small of my back once more. I soak up the heat but tell myself I'm only so conscious of it because I'm trying to distract myself. *Right.*

"Of course, of course," the maître d' replies. "Whatever you need. Thank you for coming this evening. We will see you again soon."

As soon as we're out of the stuffy air of Per Se, I feel like I can finally breathe without the thousand-pound weight of my father's memory bearing down on me, but my embarrassment is still alive and well.

That's never happened before. Ever. In eight months, nothing and no one has dragged feelings like this out of me. *So, why him? Why now?* I wish I could ask my father for guidance, and I can't help but wonder what he'd say.

"I'm so sorry. I should've just eaten the veal," I blurt out as Cannon leads me toward the elevator.

"Don't apologize. There was nothing in that restaurant I wanted to eat for dinner tonight." He shoots me a sideways glance. "Except for you."

I catch sight of my reflection in the stainless-steel doors, and my eyes are as round as saucers. Coughing on my shock, I let him lead me into the car.

"You okay?" Cannon asks, an unreadable gleam in his eyes.

I nod like a bobblehead, feeling claustrophobic in the small space alone with him.

When the doors open again at the next floor and a group of people shuffle into the elevator, I'm forced to step closer to Cannon. With his body only an inch from mine, he radiates heat like a furnace. It penetrates my dress, making me clench my legs together. *"There was nothing in that restaurant I wanted to eat for dinner tonight, except for you."*

No. Stop thinking about that. But I can't. I don't want to. Because it's the ultimate distraction from my gut punch of grief. I allow the image of him lifting me out of my seat and onto the table to spread my thighs and rip off my thong with his teeth before making a meal out of *me* to roll through my brain like frames of a perfectly filmed movie.

One of the men in the group shuffles his feet, and Cannon's hand slides around my waist, pulling me back against his hard body and away from the antsy man.

The seductive scent of cedar, bergamot, and a hint of cigar smoke wraps around me like a blanket, and my nipples peak against the bodice of my dress. *Hell. I can't handle this. Not even a little.*

I don't know how I managed to avoid smelling him

before, but now that I know he smells absolutely decadent, my body is out of control.

Wetness blooms between my legs, and I'm afraid I won't last one more floor in this elevator without turning around to attack him.

As soon as the doors open and the group spills out into the lobby, Cannon's hand drops from my belly and I rush forward, tripping over the slight gap in the floor.

Once again, he's there. Strong arms wrap around me and keep me from smashing face-first into the marble.

"Careful. You're going to give me the impression you're running from me . . . which will only make me want to chase you."

Cannon turns me in his arms, and I stare at his mouth, wishing I didn't have to hate him. Wishing this could be a real date and I didn't have hidden motives. But I do, and I always will. He doesn't even know my real name, and if I do my part right, he won't know it until I testify against him in court.

As I pull away from his hold, he glances over my shoulder and a hard look crosses his face before he pins me with his hazel eyes.

"Hold on. I have to prove a point."

I open my mouth to ask, *What?* But there's no time to get the word out.

His grip tightens around me and his lips collide with mine. When Cannon's tongue steals inside, I'm too shocked to do anything but hang on as he plunders my mouth, tasting of wine and all things forbidden.

One of his hands drags my hips closer to him, and the bulge of his erection presses against my belly.

Sweet Jesus. That can't be real.

I lose myself in the kiss, not caring that my fingernails are digging into the shoulders of his suit jacket, or that we're definitely causing a scene. At least, not until Cannon pulls back and glances over my shoulder with thunderclouds forming in his eyes.

"Come on. Let's get out of here."

I turn to see what he was looking at with such a fierce expression, but he stops me with one word.

"Don't."

What the hell did I miss?

21

CANNON

I should have expected Dom to have us tailed. Hell, I *did* expect it. But somehow, I fucking *forgot* why we were even having dinner at Per Se. Even if my lapse lasted only a few seconds, it was unforgivable.

Fuck me. I knew Drew was dangerous, but I had no clue how much until she made me forget that everything we're doing tonight is to put on a show for Dom. I also knew there was a chance he'd have someone watching us and reporting back to him so he could be sure I was telling the truth about being interested in her, and not just trying to keep her away from him.

Because even though I share his blood, I'll never have his full trust. I know that. Everyone knows it.

And even with that knowledge, I managed to let that key detail slip my mind because I'm drowning in this woman whose hand I'm gripping like a lifeline. I've never let this happen before. Ever.

When I glance at her, Drew's eyebrows strain up toward her hairline and she looks at me like I've lost my mind.

"What's going on?" she asks quietly as I pull her toward

where the Bentley idles at the curb without concern for the traffic cops giving tickets, and away from the man leaning against a lamppost only a hundred feet away.

Not just any man. *Lorenzo Angelini.* My father's number two, and someone who would be more than happy to execute an order to take me out. At least, if he could get away with it.

We're nearly the same age. Same height. Same coloring. If I hadn't been told by Dom himself that Lorenzo wasn't his son, I'd be convinced he was another bastard Casso offspring. And unless something else changes, when Dom passes on or decides to bow out, Lorenzo is the one dying to take charge of the family.

Feeling his gaze bore into the back of my head like a laser sight soon to be followed by a double tap from a .45, I pretend I didn't notice him. One thing I don't have to pretend about, though? That I want to get this woman away from here as fast as possible.

Warren alights from the Bentley as we approach and opens the back. We both slide in, and as soon as the heavy door shuts and before he can return to the driver's seat, I turn to Drew to tell her as much of the truth as I can manage, but she speaks first.

"Tanya is going to kill me, isn't she?"

I blink twice, staring at her expertly made-up face. "What the hell are you talking about?"

"Tanya. She's . . . staked her claim on you. She's going to be pissed that you kissed me." Drew scoots toward the window, as if putting distance between us.

Because she thinks I give a damn about Tanya, or that Tanya wants me? I have no idea where she got that impression, but before I can ask for an explanation, Warren slips back into the car.

117

"Where to, Mr. Freeman?" he asks with a glance in the rearview mirror.

Drew and I need more time together. Not just because of Lorenzo or because I don't understand her comment about Tanya, but also because I'm not ready to let her go tonight.

"The Halal Guys. Fifty-Third and Sixth."

Warren nods approvingly and a smile sneaks onto his face. "Yes, sir."

As soon as he pulls away from the curb and into traffic, I turn to Drew.

"What the hell are you talking about? Tanya has no claim on me."

Drew stares at me, her lower lip dropped like she's truly shocked. Her collarbones flare red and color creeps up her neck.

"But . . . but I thought you had a thing, and she wasn't over it . . . and that's why she's given me so much grief from day one. I thought that's why . . ." She trails off but her dark gaze is fixed on mine, confusion rife.

"Because you're taking her sister's job," I tell Drew, and she blinks rapidly. Once again, I catch the flicker of a lighter color in her eyes, and I open my mouth to ask her if she's wearing colored contacts, but Drew gapes at me in shock.

"This is about the *job*? And her *sister*?" With an expression that could easily be featured in an exhibit called *Mind Blown*, Drew glances from side to side, like she's piecing together everything Tanya told her from the first moment they met.

For the life of me, I can't imagine how she came to the conclusion that Tanya and I had or were having an affair. It had to be someone giving her information on me before or after she came to interview for the job, because there's no way in hell any of my staff would give her that impression.

"Yes," I reply carefully, watching her expression as I

explain. "Teal is two years younger than Tanya, whose name, by the way, was Tangerine due to her hippie mother, and Tanya changed it when she was eighteen. Don't tell her I told you that." I'm not sure why I'm giving Drew this extra information, but her shock makes me want to reassure her.

Drew's eyes widen further. "Tangerine? Oh my God. You're joking."

"No, but as you might imagine, she'll probably kill us both if she knew I told you that. Tanya and Teal didn't have the easiest life, but Teal got mixed up with the wrong people. She's more reckless, despite Tanya being wildly overprotective, because she basically raised her sister. Tanya managed to get Teal out of some trouble through sheer force of will, and when she hired on at the club, it was on the condition that Teal also be given a job."

"But if Teal wasn't a good employee . . ."

With a shrug, I give her a little more backstory as Warren changes lanes and the Bentley's thick glass mutes the horns of the cabbies just beyond the car. "I wasn't the manager of the club when they hired on. I used to . . . I had another job for a long time."

Something that looks like knowledge flickers in Drew's eyes. Wondering how much she knows about me, I test the waters.

"But you knew that, didn't you?"

It's really quite impressive to see her features turn instantly placid—like she's smoothing on a mask of indifference instead of being questioned about how much digging she did before she took her job at the Upper Ten.

"I'm not sure what you mean by that." Drew answers obliquely, her hands curling in her lap as she gives me a polite smile.

"You wouldn't have thought Tanya and I were together—

or had been—if someone hadn't given you dirt on me. You might as well tell me the rest of it, so we can find out how accurate your source was. I have a feeling you were fed a line of bullshit."

2 2

DREW

*O*h *shit. Oh hell. This isn't good.*

I don't know how Cannon has such an uncanny knack for ferreting out the truth, but his astute questions are forcing me to use my best *I have no idea what you're talking about* guise. Except, there's one big problem. Those hazel eyes of his see right through it.

I have two choices. Continue to play dumb, a technique that has worked wonders in the past. Or give him enough of the truth that he doesn't dig any further.

All it takes is one look at his face to know option two is the only real choice.

"A friend of mine. She told me everything she knew about you after I told her where I got a job. Or at least," I flick a glance at him from beneath my lashes, "everything she *thought* she knew."

Cannon leans back against the plush camel-colored leather of the luxury car and one dark eyebrow goes up. "You might as well enlighten me so I can tell you how wrong she was."

It's an invite to get more information from him, but . . . is it a trap?

I hesitate, but only for a second. If I really only knew what Randi had told me, I'd be eager to find out if it were true, so that's the role I'm going to play.

I glance down at my lap like I'm embarrassed to be having this conversation, which doesn't take any acting, *because I am*.

"She told me that you sleep with every woman who works at the club. But only one night. Only one night with *anyone*, related to the club or not." I lift my gaze to his face, and the expectant look is still there, so I continue. "She also said they all want more, but you have a strict rule and won't touch them again."

As I get the last word out, the entire cabin of the car fills with laughter, and once again, it's that full-bodied, uncaring laughter just like my father's. Cannon practically doubles over in his seat as he laughs, and from the front, Warren chimes in.

The flush I felt earlier spreads, wrapping me in embarrassment. In a small voice, I add, "I take it she wasn't completely right?"

When I look straight forward, I catch Warren's gaze in the rearview mirror as he chortles.

"Got it. Good to know." My mouth presses into a tight line as both men continue to laugh until Cannon is seconds away from needing a tissue to wipe the tears from his eyes.

"I don't know who your friend is, but I owe her a drink. Goddamn, it's been a long time since I've laughed this much."

"I'm so happy I'm able to entertain you," I tell him with my tone so brittle, it's nearly to the point of cracking.

With a shake of his head, Cannon turns to look at me. "I'm not laughing at you. Just . . . the idea that I would touch someone who worked for me—and limit myself to one night with every single woman I've ever met, if I even had time to date—is ludicrous. Your friend can't know jack shit about men."

I puff up, throwing my shoulders back, and immediately defend Randi. "I'll have you know that Downtown Randi Brown is actually quite the expert when it comes to men."

As soon as I say her name, I want to yank it back. *Oh my God. I'm a journalist. A journalist never names her source. What the hell am I thinking?* I could kick myself right out of the damn car as it goes so silent you can hear the pounding of my heart.

Cannon's expression morphs from mirthful to serious in the space of one beat. "Downtown Randi Brown, the woman who applied for a job six times, and then on the seventh, I had to tell her that there was no way she was going to work at the Upper Ten?"

"Wait. What?" The question bursts from my lips, fueled by shock.

A slight smile curves Cannon's lips once more. "Yeah, and now this explains a hell of a lot."

Inside, I'm reeling because Randi never told me about any of that. And now it makes sense. *Randi wanted to sleep with Cannon.*

"I had no idea," I whisper.

Instead of mocking me, Cannon softens his expression. "You didn't have any way to know. Randi's an interesting woman, and not one to take no for an answer."

"She calls herself a dude with tits," I say, my voice turning wooden.

Cannon coughs out another laugh. "She gets high marks for self-awareness then." He shakes his head, absorbing the information we've just exchanged, and I start to relax into the seat. "And now *I* know why she was so insistent she get the job."

Warren maneuvers the Bentley into a parking spot, and Cannon nods to the food cart on the sidewalk.

"You want to start this date over with New York's best gyros?"

Eager for a reprieve, I nod. "Absolutely."

23

CANNON

$\mathcal{W}$ e both have beef gyros wrapped in our hands when I spot a blacked-out Mercedes that looks out of place. As soon as Warren parked and let us out to get food, the Mercedes made an abrupt turn to park crooked in a loading zone across the street and about fifty feet down.

Come on, Enzo. You gotta be better than that if you want to watch me without being seen.

Then again, maybe he doesn't give a shit about stealth. Maybe he wants me to see him so I know he was given orders by Dom to make sure this date was the real thing. There's even a chance the orders didn't come from Dom. It's possible Lorenzo is trying to prove I'm full of shit, and he's the better man for the job when Dom steps down.

Either way, he's not going to get the information he's looking for.

This date, regardless of how it started out, is turning into one of the best nights I've had in years. And not only because the woman I'm with is smart, funny, and beautiful, and I want to peel that black dress off her and exhaust her in bed until she curls against me and finally lets her guard down.

But despite what Randi Brown told her, I don't shit where I eat. I never have. That lesson has been pounded into my head by Dom.

Is that why he sent Enzo for recon? Because he knows I've got a rule about never touching an employee? It would explain his skepticism and forcing us out on this date.

And now that I've spent time alone with Drew, it's only whetted my appetite for more. Good thing rules are meant to be broken.

Instead of moving back to the car where Warren waits near the back door, I lead Drew to a bench vacated by a woman who pushes her stroller down the sidewalk.

"Let's sit for a second. That dress is too pretty to end up with white sauce down the front."

Drew glances at me as we take a seat, but doesn't speak because she's still chewing on her first bite. A dab of the same white sauce I just mentioned sits just on the corner of her mouth.

"You've got a little—" I start to say, and then just decide *fuck it.*

You want to see real, Enzo? I'll show you real.

I lean forward and use my tongue to lick it off her lip.

Drew's big brown eyes, which I'm more and more convinced aren't brown at all, widen as she freezes.

"Couldn't resist," I tell her. "And it makes for a good show because we're being watched."

I have to give her credit. She doesn't panic, just relaxes her stiffened posture and leans toward me like she's going to whisper in my ear.

"By whom?"

I don't know why it's sexy to hear her use the word

126

"whom," but it is. I mimic her body position and turn toward her.

"By someone who doesn't believe what we're doing tonight is real."

Her mask, the one I've noticed she slides on and off with ease, morphs into a sweet, curious expression, one that I'd like to see on her face for real someday.

"You mean the gentleman who prompted this entire outing in the first place?"

"This one's definitely no gentleman and would like nothing more than to prove to my fath—" I almost say the word I don't allow myself to use out loud, but cut myself off. "He'd like to prove to *Frank* that I'm full of shit, because there's nothing he enjoys more than seeing me out of favor."

From her intelligent gaze, I can tell Drew picks up on exactly what I'm skating around saying.

"So, how do we prove *him* wrong?"

Her question prompts the thought I've been trying to keep out of my head since the moment she walked out of the salon at Barneys. The image of her, tangled up in my rumpled sheets, her hair a mess and her body languid.

I cut my gaze to the sidewalk, focusing on the years' worth of gum that's been ground into the concrete.

"Cannon?"

When she says my name, my attention immediately returns to her mouth. *God, what I wouldn't give to have free rein over that mouth.*

A rush of blood dives straight to my crotch, and my dick jerks against the silk lining of my suit pants.

Fuck it. It's now or never.

I stare into her eyes. "You need to spend the night with me."

24

DREW

*H*is statement leaves absolutely no room for misinterpretation, and my reaction is split into three factions.

The *holy shit, he didn't just say that* portion. The *oh my God, this is what I've been waiting for in my investigation—a chance to get into his personal space* reaction. And finally, the *I can't trust myself alone with him* piece.

It takes me three seconds to realize that not one of those parts of me is saying *no*.

I meet his hazel gaze and nod. "If that's what it takes, that's what it takes."

CANNON FREEMAN'S apartment is nothing like I anticipated. First of all, I expected Warren to take us back to a building near the club, but he doesn't. We drive a half hour across town, and instead of stopping in front of a ritzy building with a fancy address, he parks in front of a pizza shop in Little Italy.

"Thanks, Warren. We won't need you for the rest of the night. I'll text you about tomorrow."

As soon as the door shuts on the Bentley, it disappears, and we're left standing on a sidewalk amidst the scent of oregano, basil, and tomatoes, with lights strung along awnings, lending a hint of romance to the atmosphere.

"My place is upstairs."

Somehow, I find my fingers twining into Cannon's as he pulls me along behind him to a heavy red steel door.

Instantly, all I can picture is Christian Grey's red room, and a flush, like I've just chugged a carafe of wine, steals over me. *Nothing about this feels fake. It feels as real as a date gets.*

Thankfully, Cannon is busy unlocking the three dead bolts with a key and opening the door rather than noticing I'm overheated with thoughts of him telling me I'm going to be a good girl for him or I'll be punished.

Oh my God. Where did that come from?

My brain seems to have been hijacked from my own control, because I'm not feeling like myself at all right now. I force myself to note every single detail about the place, from the gray-painted concrete entryway to the wide opening of the industrial elevator.

"It's not fancy, but it's mine," he says as he moves the gates and waves me into the car.

"The elevator's yours?" I say, joking, but my question falls flat when he nods and unlocks the black metal gate.

"Yeah, the whole building is. It was the only way I could save Geno from getting evicted. I'm pretty fucking partial to his pizza, so I did what I had to do."

I gape at Cannon. The cost of owning any apartment in New York City is pretty much astronomical, but to own a whole building?

Holy shit.

"You own a building?"

"A few buildings, actually." He punches a long code into a security panel in the elevator, and then we move upward. "When the bottom fell out of the real estate market along with the financial crash, I made some smart investments."

He meets my gaze, and I'm sure my shock is written all over my face.

"You do know that I used to be the COO of Karas International and worked with Creighton Karas for over a decade, right? Randi would've had to tell you that, especially because it's no secret."

"Yeah, but . . . I didn't realize . . ." I trail off as we slowly rise toward the top floor.

"That I might've been a damn good businessman? Because I am. It's all right, though. I'm used to being underestimated. I prefer it most of the time. It's much easier to maneuver around people when everyone just thinks you're skating through life on connections rather than on your merit."

In that moment, I see Cannon Freeman in a completely different light than I have since the day I walked into the Upper Ten. He's not just the illegitimate son of one of the most notorious mobsters in modern times. He's *real*.

And that's insanely dangerous.

When the elevator rocks to a stop, he opens the gate once more and indicates for me to precede him to exit. I step onto a wood floor of wide planks stained an ashy gray. The worn grooves in the wood tell me that it's probably original to the building but has been cared for in recent years. There are two heavy metal doors, both painted black, and the interior walls are a grayish, almost whitewashed brick.

Cannon points to one door. "Emergency stairs, if the elevator isn't working or you can't get into it." I assume he adds the last part because he had to unlock the gate for us to even use the elevator. "But the emergency stairs are locked on the stairwell side. You can always get down, but you can't get up unless you've been invited."

It's not hard to imagine what kind of security concerns he deals with on a regular basis to make sure his home is locked up tight. As Dom Casso's bastard son, he has to feel like he walks around with a target on his back at all times.

"Makes sense," I say and turn toward the other door. "And I assume this is your place?"

"Yeah, this is home." He uses another key to open the dead bolts and leans inside to stop the beeping of the alarm.

When he pushes open the door, I'm not sure what to expect. Maybe something glass and metal and übermodern and masculine, but that's not the case at all. It's absolutely stunning, to be sure, but also completely charming.

The same whitewashed brick lines the walls. Ductwork, painted charcoal gray to match the steel beams, is exposed beneath the soaring white ceiling. The same scarred ash-gray plank floor extends inside, covered by what look like hand-woven rugs. A gray fabric sectional curves around a cement table, and some of the cushions have permanent indents from wear.

It's not new. It's not chic. But it's perfect. And he's right. It looks like home, which is a far cry from my sterile, bland apartment that serves only as a staging ground for my mission.

"This is incredible," I say, turning in a slow circle to take in the clean lines and yet completely inviting atmosphere. Massive houseplants take up residence in the corners, and the windows extend from floor to ceiling.

I wander over to a happy-looking bamboo as Cannon hangs his keys near the door with a jangle.

Night drapes over Little Italy like a blanket, and the lights of the shops and restaurants glow from below us. Across the street, the windows are dark, waiting for their residents to come home from work or play. It's a perfect little haven from the busy movement of the rest of the city.

Cannon's scent wraps around me, telling me he's right behind me. "I'm glad you like it."

I turn to face him, eminently aware of my chest being only inches from his. "Who wouldn't like it?"

"No one I'd let come here." His eyes are hooded as he stares down at my face.

"Is this really making our date more realistic if you don't usually bring women here?" I ask as once again, everything happening between us feels totally genuine and not staged.

One corner of Cannon's mouth lifts. "I didn't say I don't bring women here. Just . . . not many." The warmer colors of his ever-changing hazel eyes heat as they roam over my face. "Bringing you here is a definite statement, though. One that can't be misinterpreted."

The glass cooling my back is at direct odds with the warmth of his body radiating against my front.

"When's the last time you made a statement like this?" I ask, my attention fixed on his third button, even though I didn't intend to voice the question.

Cannon waits until my gaze meets his before he replies. "Jealous? Like you were of Tanya getting a piece of me?"

Mulish stubbornness dictates that I reply with a decisive, "No. Not at all."

"Liar," Cannon whispers as he leans forward and sweeps his lips across mine. "Kiss me back."

I know I shouldn't kiss him. That's not why I'm here. I should be finding a way to sneak off and snoop through anything that could possibly help me find dirt that will bring down his family. But when his lips drift across mine again, I can't resist.

They're soft and warm, and I want more.

My thought from earlier comes back. Cannon Freeman is the ultimate distraction. As soon as I open my mouth to him and his tongue sweeps inside to stroke mine, I can't think of anything but him. All other thought is obliterated from my mind.

There's only the heat of his body as he pulls me closer against him. The strength of his arms as they wrap around me, anchoring me to him in a statement that can't be misunderstood.

He wants me as much as I want him. Even though I tell myself to push him away, to remember this isn't for real, that this isn't something I'm supposed to enjoy . . . I can't. I'm totally lost in him.

It should terrify me, but I'm too busy tilting my head to give him better access to take the kiss deeper. His hand grips my ass and the other curls around my face, keeping me where he wants me.

It's the most erotic kiss of my entire life. I'm seconds away from wrapping my leg around his waist when something vibrates against me, and it's not the buzz of his arousal. It's his phone.

"Shit." He pulls away an inch with a curse and fishes his cell from his pocket. "One second. Let me shut this off."

I step back, out of his arms, and try to calm my hammering heart. "No, answer it. It's fine."

I turn and walk toward the charcoal-gray matte kitchen cabinets and the black sink. Even though this isn't my place, I open the cupboards until I find a thick glass, then fill it with water from the tap to gulp it down like it's going to somehow change what just happened.

I kissed him. I want him. I'm so fucked.

Before my mental flagellation can ramp up, Cannon's phone starts buzzing again.

"Freeman. What?"

I can't hear the other side of the conversation, and I should be kicking myself for not staying close enough to listen in, but I'm gulping down water like it's the elixir that will save me from making more bad decisions.

"What the fuck is he doing there?" Cannon spins to face the window, pressing his palm on the whitewashed brick between the floor-to-ceiling panes. "He doesn't have a meeting with me, and the only reason he's fucking there— Never mind. Tell him I'm not going to be in tonight. He knows why. No. He can't call me. I'm turning my phone off. I'm unavailable for the night. You can handle it, Grice. Yeah. Yeah. Night."

Cannon pushes off the wall, stalks to the coffee table near the sectional, and tosses his phone onto a stack of newspapers. He jams his hand into his hair, and the shorter pieces stand up on end when he finally looks to where I'm standing in the kitchen, clutching my glass like it's the Holy Grail.

"Everything okay?" I ask because I think he's waiting for me to inquire, but also because I'm crazy curious about who could be at the club that would piss him off so much.

"Lorenzo. The prick who was following us earlier. He showed up at the club and wanted to meet with me."

"But he knows you're not at the club."

Cannon shakes his head and looks sideways. "I never said he was a mental giant. He probably thought he was being tricky. Asking if I was at the club, so I wouldn't think he was following us. Seriously sloppy work."

I lower the empty glass to the counter. "Isn't it useful,

though? Now he knows for sure you're not leaving tonight? Doesn't that mean we're in the clear?"

"You in a hurry to leave?" Cannon's gaze cuts to my face as he asks the question, and a flush creeps up my chest and spreads over my shoulders.

"Is there a chance they're going to be watching your place, waiting for me to leave?"

One leisurely step at a time, Cannon crosses the apartment to come toward me. "If I say no, how fast will you be out the door?" He stops on the opposite side of the kitchen bar and waits for my answer while my brain goes haywire.

It's now or never. Stay or go. Fight or flight.

The logical part of me says my investigation would be better served by my staying, but I'm lying to myself if I claim that's the only reason swaying my decision.

It's not.

I want to stay for purely selfish reasons. I want to stay because I want to spend more time with this man who makes me feel things I haven't felt in years . . . if ever.

But I can't say what I'm thinking. I don't know how.

So instead, I press my lips together and meet his eyes. "I'd hate to do anything that doesn't fit the story you've set in motion."

25

CANNON

I know when a woman wants me, and it's been a long time since I've wanted one this badly. Drew is afraid to come out and ask for what she wants. Something about that softens the tension that snapped into place in my spine as soon as Grice told me who'd showed up at the club asking for me.

As a matter of fact, it all drains away as I recall how fucking sweet she was pressed against me. I want more of her, and I want her now. But from the way she's clutching the empty glass, I can tell Drew's skittish. That can be fixed.

"You want a drink?"

She glances down at the one she's holding.

"Not water. Wine. Scotch. Whiskey. Vodka. Name your poison."

She drank wine at dinner, but something about her tells me that's not her only beverage of choice.

The corners of her lips curl up. "You have any bourbon?"

"Picked up a bottle of Four Roses the other day."

The beginnings of a smile bloom into a full one. "That's my favorite, actually."

"Then Four Roses it is."

I back away from the kitchen to the antique industrial metal cabinet I saw at a flea market that used to grace the office of some factory back in the day. It had a padlock still on it, and I used a lock pick to open it rather than cut it off, because of some sentimental reason I still can't put into words. I use the lock as a paperweight on my desk in my office now, despite the fact it gets rust on everything beneath it.

The cage-looking door swings open on well-oiled hinges when I pull on the metal handle. My stuff might not be the newest or the nicest, but I take care of what's mine.

"One finger or two?" I ask, turning to watch her blush rise further. I'm not disappointed as it spreads until it disappears under the shoulders of her dress and beneath the thick layer of makeup.

Just as I start to think I want to wipe her face clean so I can see her blush stain her cheeks, she surprises me with an impish smirk.

"I'm a three-finger kind of girl. Especially in situations like this."

I can't help but grin at her response. "I knew there was something special about you."

I turn back to fill antique cut-crystal glasses with three fingers of bourbon each and carry them to the counter of the kitchen bar. I offer one to her, and she wraps her palm around it.

"To an unexpected night," I say, lifting my glass in salute.

She does the same, tapping the heavy base against mine. "To a very unexpected night."

We both sip the smooth, mellow bourbon. The spice washes over my tongue, followed by a hint of pear and apple.

Drew lowers her glass from her lips with an appreciative

sigh. "God, that's always so good. No wonder my dad refused to drink anything else." As soon as she makes the comment, her entire body freezes, like she didn't mean to say it.

She mentioned my laugh reminded her of someone at dinner, and I'm willing to bet this entire building on the fact that it was her dad. The dad she lost.

"What was he like?"

I ask the question, and Drew shrinks into herself for a few beats before lifting the glass to take another long drink. When she finally finds the courage to meet my gaze again, her eyes glisten.

"He was a good man." She swallows like there's a lump caught in her throat from her husky words. "A really good man."

"I take it he passed?"

She nods solemnly. "Too soon. Much too soon."

"I'm sorry, Drew. The good ones always go too soon."

She blinks a few times and looks up, like she's trying to stop the tears from falling. Again, I see that flicker of color beneath what I'm now certain is a colored contact lens.

But if I ask her about them right now, that would make me a huge dick. So instead, with my glass in hand, I cross back to the liquor cabinet and grab the bottle. "Come on, I want to show you something."

Quietly, Drew follows me through the loft from the kitchen and living room area into my private domain—my office.

Inside, the two towering front and back walls are covered completely by bookshelves stacked with classics and first editions I've picked up individually or bought in bulk online. I bypass those to stop in front of the antique shuffleboard lane mounted next to the wall of windows that start at waist height and span upward about ten feet.

"Want to play?" I ask, but she's too busy taking in the rest of the room to focus on the game.

"This is incredible."

Her gaze sweeps over my desk, from the same old factory as the liquor cabinet, to the massive wingback chair in the corner with an Edison bulb pendant shining down on the spot where I try to carve out time to read every day. It was a habit Dom started me on when he handed me *The Art of War* when I was twelve and told me to memorize it, which is probably the only reason I've lived as long as I have.

"This is the inner sanctum. No one else comes here. Ever."

She finally turns to the industrial farmhouse-style shuffleboard table, her eyes wide. "Then who do you play against?"

"Myself. Unless you're willing to give me a real competitor."

For a moment, I think she's going to say no, and I'm coming up with arguments to change her mind. But instead of shaking her head, she kicks off her heels and crosses the wood floor barefoot.

"I don't know about being a real competitor, but I'll at least save you from playing like you're an only child. Lord knows that sucked as a kid for me fairly often." She lifts her dark eyes to mine. "What about for you?"

It's the first time she's asked me about my childhood, a subject people avoid like the bubonic plague if they know who my father is. Since I haven't outright admitted it to Drew yet, I decide it's time.

I set my bourbon on the windowsill and stare out at the buildings across the street. "My mother tried to make things as normal as she could, but it was hard when she was constantly trying to regain Dom's attention and affection for herself. She basically chased him away a few years after I was born. In case you haven't put it together, Dom is my father."

As soon as the words are out, I wonder if I've made a mistake. I never admit who Dom truly is to me, either verbally, in writing, or otherwise.

Thankfully, Drew doesn't gasp in shock, something I probably have Randi to thank for, because I can't imagine she wouldn't fill Drew in on that piece of information.

"It sounds like he didn't need to be chased away, because he's an old tomcat, too busy trotting from alley to alley to remember who he left behind," she says, and I turn to catch her shrug with an apologetic smile. "Sorry, I probably shouldn't have said that."

I shake my head, gripping the neck of the bottle. "It's fine. It's all ancient history now. It's actually refreshing to be able to talk about it. I don't get the chance often. Or rather, there aren't many people who wouldn't take that information and spread it around in a way that would come back and bite me in the ass."

26

DREW

I've never felt guilt for lying before. Never felt guilt for ferreting out information that needs to come to light. But with Cannon Freeman, a man who may possibly have done unspeakable things, I feel the curling claws of regret digging into my belly when I think about what I can do with the information he's sharing freely with me.

I want to open my mouth and tell him not to trust me. Tell him to stop talking about anything that matters or could hurt him.

But I can't.

Because that would undoubtedly get me killed, and an untimely death isn't in my plans for tonight.

So I do the only other thing that might allay my conscience. I share things with him that I have no business sharing.

"My father was my best friend. He was brilliant, but so humble. The reason I love working at the club is because sometimes I catch a hint of the cigars, and it reminds me of the ones he'd sit outside and smoke while my mother poured a bottle of vodka down her gullet."

I lift my gaze to meet Cannon's hazel eyes, wondering if he can see how bare and vulnerable that admission is from me.

"How did he die?" Cannon asks, and pain swipes through me like a hot knife through butter.

The question is a brutal reminder of why I'm here.

I hold out my glass. "I'm going to need a lot more bourbon for that."

"Come and get it, because you look like I need to kiss you again."

Instantly, the sadness enveloping me dissipates into a fluttering flock of butterflies trying to escape my chest.

How does he do this to me? Even though I wasn't sure how to respond, my feet move across the planks of hardwood toward him, as if drawn by an eerie magnetic force.

Maybe that's the explanation for all of this. I'm drawn to Cannon Freeman in a way I've never been drawn to another man before. My entire goal was to bring him down when I topple the Casso family empire, but now, I can't help but hope that there's a way I can save him from the aftermath if he's innocent.

My instincts can't be that wrong, can they? Cannon couldn't have had anything to do with my father's death.

Stop it. Now you're talking crazy.

Even as my thoughts are being torn in opposite directions, I hear the click of my glass as I set it on the ledge of the window, and my body fits against Cannon's like this is where I've always been meant to stand.

"I have so many questions for you," he says in a husky tone. "But as much as I want answers, I want your mouth more."

I meet his heated gaze with the knowledge that my barriers are falling and my instinct for self-preservation is fading much too quickly. "I want to tell you things I shouldn't," I whisper, my lips only a breath from his. "But I want you to kiss me more."

In that moment, I give him a part of myself I haven't given anyone else since my last conversation with my father —total honesty.

I don't know who closes the distance, but our lips collide and arousal zips through me like a lightning bolt. I wrap my leg around his hip, and the hard bulge of his erection presses against me. I moan, hell, maybe I purr, as his hand cups my ass and pulls me closer to wedge his hips between the *V* of my legs.

His lips drop from my mouth to my throat as he uses his other hand to tug my hair backward—by my wig.

Fuck!

I jerk away, and Cannon stares at me like I've grown a second head.

Arousal circles the drain to be replaced by hard chips of ice in his eyes. My heart pounds in my throat, choking off my quick and easy explanations, and I stand here gaping at him like a fish out of water.

In a voice that demands the truth, Cannon grinds out, "Why are you wearing a wig and colored contacts? What the fuck else are you hiding?"

Stay cool. Act cool. Be cool.

I've prepared for this, I remind myself. *I have a plan. Get it together. Laugh it off.*

But I don't want to lie to Cannon anymore, which is probably the dumbest thought I've had in my entire life. Honesty will get me killed; of that, I have no doubt. But summoning the lies to my lips is like chewing glass. I can't speak them to his face, so I drop my gaze to the floor.

"I . . . Randi told me you liked dark-eyed blondes. I . . . I thought it would make it easier to get the job if you liked looking at me."

The heavy silence threatens to suck all the oxygen from the room as I study the striations in the wood beneath my bare feet and wait for judgment to be cast.

"Take it off." The order comes out on a growl as Cannon's black leather loafers come into view.

The urge to shrink away and run is so strong, I almost can't force myself to look him in the eye again. Somehow, I manage.

The pale green flames of his hazel eyes burn with such intensity that they threaten to singe me.

"Why?"

"I want to see you," he says, ducking down to force me to hold his gaze. "The real you."

With trembling fingers, I reach up to tug at the pins holding the wig in place and slide it off my head, taking the wig liner with it. I'm left with my long hair clipped flat to the back of my head.

I know I could have told him no, told him it's none of his damn business if I wanted to wear a wig. But part of me wants him to see me too. The real me. The me that no one ever sees.

Even when I would report on the air, I wore a wig. In my entire life, I've never appeared in front of a camera without changing my appearance. It was my father's biggest regret about his career—that it completely stole his privacy. He couldn't go anywhere without being recognized, and he didn't want the same for me.

I listened and I learned, stealing my stepmother's wigs from when she was recovering from breast cancer years before. In minutes, I could look like someone else. And over the years, I got so good at it that sometimes I forgot who the real me was.

But one by one, I pull the clips from my hair, forming a stack next to my glass, and let my loosened hair fall around my shoulders until all the clips are gone. Finally, I shake out my dark brown locks and meet his eyes once more. I'm not sure what I was expecting to see there, but instead of judgment, I see curiosity and . . . appreciation.

"Randi lied to you, Drew. This is so much better."

Because I'm already in for a penny, I reach up and quickly snatch the contacts from my eyes, revealing piercing aqua-blue irises that I've missed seeing in the mirror.

That's when Cannon stumbles back a step. "Jesus Christ. How could you cover those?"

The truth, that eyes like mine are too memorable for people to easily forget me, hangs on my tongue, but I can't give that to him. No matter how much I wish I could.

"It sounded like a good idea at the time."

I back away from him, heading for my purse to stick the contacts in the case before returning.

Cannon steps forward and runs the pad of his thumb along my jaw. "One day, I'm going to wake up next to you and see only *you*. It's going to be the most beautiful sight of my life."

My knees threaten to give out as his vow wraps around me. Instead of trying to support myself, I give in to my desire and reach for Cannon.

"Kiss me. Make me believe you really want that."

Another lie, because I know he wants that. There's no way he can stare at me like this without his words being anything but sincere. And I don't know if I have the willpower to resist his fantasy coming true *tomorrow*.

I want him.

But it's not safe to trust him completely, because I can't trust anyone completely.

Still, that doesn't mean I can't take what little bit of this I can steal. Later, I'll have the memories, when I no longer have him in my life.

Cannon doesn't hesitate. His lips are on mine. His tongue delves deep and twines, tangling with mine. But that's not what sends me over the edge. No, it's the way his hands thread through my hair, tugging at the strands and turning me from one angle to the next.

My arms wrap around his neck, and it's all I can do to keep myself from climbing him. Cannon lifts me off the floor, but I don't know where we're moving until something firm brushes against my ass and I'm seated with him between my legs.

When he pulls away, I blink, trying to place myself in his office. That's when I realize I'm seated on his desk and he's dropping into his chair in front of me.

Cannon's gaze burns into me as he drags it from where his hands grip my knees until it lands on my face. "Remember what I said in the restaurant?"

His words fly back into my head, because how could I possibly forget him saying I was the only thing he wanted to eat at Per Se.

I nod, my desire climbing higher with the hemline of my dress, which he pushes up inch by inch.

With a wicked grin, he stops when he sees the black thong covering me. He sweeps the pad of his thumb over my center, and a full-body shiver works through me. I've never felt *need* like this. Achingly. Desperately. The look on his face tells me that I won't be going unsatisfied.

And his words confirm it.

"I don't touch the people who work for me, but I can't

stop with you. Not unless you tell me to back the fuck off and stay away. I'll keep coming back. I don't know why, but there's something I can't fucking resist. I know I should, but I don't want to."

When I reach down and wrap my hand around his forearm, Cannon's entire body stills, like he's expecting me to push him away. But that's the opposite of what I have planned.

"Whatever you do, please don't stop. I . . . I need this. I need you."

Cannon's nostrils flare at the raw and honest words. Somehow, I know in that moment, that's all he wants from me. *Honesty.*

I send up a promise to the universe. *Someday I'll tell him why. I'll tell him all of it. Just . . . not yet.*

With my conscience temporarily satisfied, I lean back on the empty desk, balancing on my elbows as he catches the fabric between my legs with a hooked finger, right in the vicinity of where I'd prefer to have him buried inside me, and pulls it a breath away from my body.

"Baby, you're soaked." Cannon's bourbon-warmed voice takes on a husky, awed quality as he realizes how hungry I am for him. "These panties are a lost cause. We'd better take them off."

With hunger for him driving through my veins, I lift my hips as he uses both hands to drag my panties over my generous ass and down my thighs until I kick them off my feet.

And then it's just him staring—at me, completely exposed —and the pulse already pounding in my ears goes haywire.

"Fuck, you're so pretty here." With the slightest sweep up, the pad of his thumb slips through my wetness and I squirm against the desk, wanting more from him.

I rock my hips forward, forcing his touch to deepen, and a wicked grin steals onto his lips.

"Oh no. You're not going to fuck my fingers until I'm ready to give them to you." His hazel eyes ignite with challenge as they lift to meet mine. "You're used to being in charge, but that's not how it's going to be with me. Not when I'm staring at the prettiest pussy I've ever seen. I'm going to take my time with you. If you can't handle that, I'll make you handle it. Get me?"

Hell. Why is that the sexiest thing I've ever heard? My brain is rioting in approval, but my lips press together, and some proper part of me is afraid to agree out loud.

Cannon must see my inner struggle, because he grips both my knees and rises until he and I are face-to-face. "Are you going to be able to handle it? Or do I need to strap you down to the desk to keep you where I want you?"

Another burst of heat lights up between my legs, and I have to be dripping onto the surface of the desk.

"I . . . I don't know." What I want wars with what I think I should say, but he sees through it. Through me.

"Poor little girl. You haven't ever had a man like me. I bet the rest of them let you decide when and where and how much and how hard." He grips my chin between his thumb and forefinger and leans forward to nip at my lips. "That's not how I work."

"Why?" I ask, my voice trembling.

"You don't know what you want from me because you've never had a man determined to set you on fire, just so I can fan the flames. I'm going to show you."

With his hands still locked around my knees, he lifts my right leg until my foot is resting on the edge of the desk and then the left. I'm exposed. Obscenely exposed. Looking at his handiwork, he sits back down and reaches forward to pull my ass closer to the edge.

"Heaven," he murmurs before he bends forward and sweeps his tongue through my slit, ass to clit, and groans so loud, the vibrations nearly set off an orgasm by themselves.

"Oh my God," I whisper. My fingers curl into claws as I try to grab onto anything that'll help me keep quiet. But there's nothing other than the fists they ball into as Cannon goes back for more and *devours*.

Holy Jesus. Cannon's tongue is a gift to womankind. He tastes and licks and teases until I'm fighting his grip on my hips. He's trying to keep me pinned to the desk, and I'm desperate to push my pussy harder into his face because my orgasm is *right there*. So damn close. But he won't let me have it.

"You taste fucking delicious." He groans as he goes back for more. Except this time, he adds two fingers that press inside me and scissor, stretching me until I can't stop myself from fucking them.

"Please. Please, just—"

But he isn't taking orders from me, just like he said. He's drawing it out and making me crazy while sparks burst along the edge of my vision, and I'm grasping for what remains just out of reach.

"So close. Please."

My begging tips it over the edge. When Cannon's teeth close lightly around my clit and his fingers press right where I need them, I explode with a scream.

The orgasm washes over me, staying strong as he stokes the flames higher, but I'm insensible. My head whips back and forth as I ride it out, never wanting it to end.

At least, not until he says, "That a girl, Drew. Good girl."

Drew.

Drew.

Drew.

My fake name clangs like a warning bell, dragging me out of pleasure and back into reality.

Fuck. What am I doing? I scramble back up to a sitting position, my chest heaving, and Cannon Freeman's face, the face of my target and enemy, inches from my pussy.

It's safe to say that this definitely isn't how my investigation was supposed to go.

27

CANNON

*T*here's a shift in Drew that I can't explain, but it's almost like her orgasm scared the hell out of her. Now, instead of pressing into me for more, she's trying to move away.

I'm not a stupid man, and her explanation for the wig and contacts was weak. There's something she's not telling me, and her reaction now is even more evidence of it.

Drew Carson isn't who she seems.

What she wants, I don't know, but I'll find out. If I have to, I'll cuff her to my bed and make her come over and over from the most erotic kind of torture I can dream up, until her final wall crumbles.

But with that soft, hazy look on her face right now, I don't want to spook her more. I want to hold her close and see how she reacts to someone taking care of her.

Given the amount of blood pulsing in my crotch, I'm amazed I'm still capable of logical thought at the moment. Call it my superpower.

Instead of pushing her more right now, when I can practically see her walls slamming down, I roll away from the desk so she can shut her legs, but after an inch, I pause.

"I want to get one thing straight right now. This has nothing to do with what happens at the club or whatever reason you really felt the need to wear a wig and contacts. This is between us. Get me?"

Drew nods quickly, and I roll the rest of the way back.

As I stand, I place one hand on the desk on either side of her hips so our noses are an inch apart.

"That will not be the last time I eat your pussy. I'll promise you that. Now, come on. You owe me that game of shuffleboard we just got distracted from."

AN HOUR LATER, I know I should have thrown Drew out of my apartment immediately after I wiped the taste of her from my lips.

Her laughter fills my office as she fucking beats me at the game I play almost every day by myself, and the sight of joy on her face is absolutely fucking breathtaking.

When I said she was dangerous, I didn't even know the extent of her powers of devastation.

"We really should've played for money. Because I do believe I just crushed you again." Drew points to her shuffle-board weights, which sit in the area that is awarded the most points.

"How in the hell are you able to keep doing that?" The incredulity in my tone speaks for itself.

Drew's grin grows wider as she laughs. "You told me to take it easy, and I am. Otherwise, I'd have been overshooting for the last hour instead of kicking your ass. So really, it's your fault."

I stalk around the shuffleboard lane, and as soon as she realizes my intent, her teeth click together and she backs up two steps.

"Hey, whoa. Whatever you're planning right now . . . slow your roll, big man. Don't want to be a sore loser."

When I fake like I'm going to charge at her, she bolts for the door, exactly as I expected. I cut her off and grab her around the waist, lifting her into the air before she can get away.

"I declare myself the winner, and *you* are my prize," I say as she squirms in my grip.

"Not fair!" she shrieks, trying to wiggle free.

I walk out of my office, toward the broken-in sectional in the living room as I easily fend off her attempts. Readjusting her in my hold, I lower her to the cushions and drop my full body weight on top of her. Pinned beneath me, Drew tries to escape, and her dark hair is a wild mess.

"You're not going anywhere. Not until I let you."

She stills at my words and stares into my eyes.

The blue-green color I've only ever seen in the waters of the Caribbean still takes my breath away. Her eyes are like a gut punch to the soul. They heat like she's now thinking of things that have nothing to do with getting away from me.

Her top teeth dig into her bottom lip. "What are you claiming for your ill-gotten gains?"

I lean down and steal a kiss. "You."

"What part of me?" she asks, sounding almost breathless.

"All of you."

Oh Christ. That's not fair. He can't say things like that to me. Because now my insides are melting, I have no panties to block the flood of wetness between my thighs, and I want to crawl out from under him and ride him until neither of us remembers our names. *Real or fake.*

And the way he looks at me . . . no one has ever looked at me like that.

Like he can't see what I'm hiding, but he knows there's something and just doesn't care—because he wants me, secrets and all. Okay, so maybe I'm projecting that piece because I desperately want it to be true. Even though I know that this can end nowhere good. *Right?*

Unless . . . Cannon Freeman spent most of his adult life on the right side of the law, working for Creighton Karas. It's only been since Karas fired him that he's been running the Upper Ten, which is technically also on the right side of the law, regardless of the mob meetings that take place there. But those could happen anywhere, right? That wouldn't make him a criminal purely by association, would it? At most, maybe an accomplice of some kind?

My brain is working overtime here, trying to come up with all the reasons why I can still complete my investigation and take down the Casso family . . . but keep Cannon out of the cross fire. So I can keep *him*.

I'm crazy. Absolutely insane. This is the worst plan in the history of plans, and my father would tell me that you can't ride two horses with one ass.

But this man is special. It isn't his fault he was born the bastard son of a mob boss. He can still be a good man. Right?

There's no one else in my head to agree or argue with my rationale, so I arbitrarily decide my instincts are on point and give myself permission to do exactly what I want to do right now. I maneuver until we've changed positions, with Cannon on the bottom and me kneeling between his knees on the cushion.

My fingers slide into the waistband of his suit pants and his hard, flat stomach sucks in, as though he's shocked I'm touching him there.

"Drew . . ."

When he says my fake name, I block it out. I don't want him to call me that. I want him to call me by my real name.

Someday, I promise myself silently.

"Shush. If you're going to be a caveman and declare yourself the winner despite the fact that I won, you should accept the spoils I offer." I look up at him from under my eyelashes. "My mouth."

Cannon's lips form the word *fuck* silently as I free the button and tug at the zipper. We both say it out loud when his thick, hard cock springs forward into my hand.

Oh God.

I didn't expect his penis to be just as beautiful as every other part of him, but I probably should have.

It's got girth and is well-formed—long and thick and just

155

slightly curved toward his belly. The head takes on a dusky reddish-purple hue, and a little pearl-sized drop of clear fluid drips from the end.

I can't help it. I lap it up, loving the salty flavor.

Cannon shoves his pants down further and groans. "*Fuck. God. Yes.*"

I wrap my palm around him and squeeze, milking more from him to lap up like it's my prize. He widens his knees and lifts upward, bringing his cock to my mouth, and slides it against my lips. "Can you take me?"

I reach out and tap the head with my tongue. "I can try."

And with that, he pushes forward, his cock tunneling between my lips, and I take him halfway, sucking hard as he pulls back.

"Jesus. I need to fuck your face."

My thighs squeeze together, and I nod. "I want that too."

He lifts up and powers into my mouth. I take him deeper and easier with each stroke, and Cannon's face contorts with pleasure.

"Fuck. Fuck. Fuck."

He's fighting the urge to come, and selfishly, I want to push him over the edge, into the oblivion that I couldn't resist when he was stealing my control.

Finally, he tries to pull away, but I move forward, sucking him deeper. He finds my hand, squeezing it tight as he throws his head back and roars. His cock pulses in my mouth and I swallow eagerly, proud that I could take him to the same place he took me.

The next time he attempts to move, I release my hold on him and his cock slides out of my mouth. Cannon tucks himself back into his pants before pulling me up his body so my head lies on his chest, listening as his heart pounds like a jackhammer.

"Jesus fuck. I didn't expect that. Didn't—"

"Shut up and enjoy the afterglow," I tell him as I press a kiss to his stubbled jaw.

* * *

I TOLD myself I wasn't going to do it. I told myself not to take the risk. Shockingly, I lied.

As soon as Cannon's breathing turns even in the living room, I slip out of the bed he insisted that I take for myself and silently creep across his apartment.

Sounds from the city invade—sirens, horns, car alarms, yelling—and I'm thankful for all of them because I'm hoping they hide my movements.

As I slip into Cannon's office, I tell myself that the keystroke logger is going to prove him innocent, and not give me more information to make my case.

This could save him.

But my guilt still rages.

I can't help but ask myself—*why now?* After all of the people I've become to get the stories I broke for the world and the justice that followed, why am I now developing such an overbearing conscience?

I slip the flash drive into the port on the side of his laptop and wait the thirty seconds it takes for the software to do its job. When it's done, I pull it out again and tiptoe through the living room, praying I can get back to the bedroom without him knowing. As soon as I hit the doorway, it's obvious no one is answering my prayers tonight.

A light flips on in the kitchen area, coming from the fridge. I spin around to face it and freeze.

Cannon stands there, a bottle of water tipped toward his lips, staring at me. He lowers the bottle, his gaze sweeping

from the top of my mussed hair to the toes of my bare feet—
and every naked inch in between.

"You walk around my apartment like that in the middle of
the night, and I'm going to take it as an invitation to come
put you back to bed and stay there with you."

There is literally nothing I'd prefer more at this moment,
even with the flash drive clutched tightly in my hand.

"Then why don't you come join me?" The words fall from
my lips without thought.

Cannon doesn't miss a beat. He closes the fridge and the
light extinguishes.

"You're not ready for that. But next time you ask, I won't
say no." In the darkness, his deep voice sounds even more
menacing as he delivers the promise. "Go to bed, Drew.
We've got a lot to talk about in the morning."

DREW

*T*he next morning, I do what all cowards do when they realize they've gotten in too deep—I run.

Cannon is asleep on the couch as I sneak out of his apartment. Cringing at the clanging of the elevator, I shove my wig back on my head and hold my breath until I'm out of the building and on the sidewalk, doing the walk of shame in last night's dress.

I don't know what he wanted to talk about this morning, but I know that I'm not emotionally equipped for any conversation with him right now.

Thumbing the app on my phone, I receive confirmation that my ride will be arriving within two minutes, and I hope it's fast enough to escape before Cannon realizes that I'm gone.

As I stand on the sidewalk, a strange feeling pricks at me, and I glance to the right and across the street to an open car window and notice a cloud of cigarette smoke—coming straight out of a face I've seen before.

GTR. The younger Rossetti from the meeting at the Upper Ten. Hell. That's not good.

I drop my attention to my phone, pretending I'm engrossed in watching the car on its way to get me as it loops around blocks and waits at lights. In reality, I'm silently chanting *hurry up, hurry up, hurry up.*

Because now I'm caught between a rock and an awkwardly hard place. I'm going to have to tell Cannon who I saw as I was sneaking out of his apartment.

Not that the awkwardness wasn't going to happen anyway, since I have to work tomorrow and he'll most likely be there.

But can the Rossetti information wait that long?

Finally, the longest two minutes of my life end, and the car with the sign for the ride-share app posted in the back window pulls up along the sidewalk. I check the face of the driver and compare it to the one on the screen. It all matches, along with the make and model of the car, so I climb in.

Thankfully, he doesn't try to make any small talk and focuses on driving, which leaves me to my thoughts and trying to decide if I should tell Cannon right now or wait.

Fuck it. I'm not going to put him in possible danger in a *mob rivalry* because I'm a chickenshit who couldn't stay to face him in the morning.

I use the phone number Cannon gave me for emergencies when I started at the club and type out a text.

ME: *I'm really sorry, I had to run. Thought you should know that as I was waiting for my ride, I saw a guy sitting in a car who looked like someone from the meeting the other night. The younger one from the R family.*

I STARE DOWN at my text and decide that my attempt at being

subtle leaves a lot to be desired, but I don't know how else to give him the information. Before I can second-guess myself more, I hit SEND, hoping like hell Cannon is still asleep and I won't have to deal with replying to him until much later in the day.

My entire body jerks as my phone vibrates in my hand.

CANNON: *You're not stealthy or quiet. Come back up.*

ME: *Sorry, already on my way home.*

CANNON: *Then I'll come to you.*

ME: *He's watching your apartment. Do you really think that's a good idea?*

THE RAPID-FIRE TEXT exchange comes to a halt when I don't get a reply from Cannon, and I can only imagine what he's doing. I can picture him walking across the street, naked, his dick swinging as he yanks GTR from the car and drags him inside to interrogate him.

Okay, so maybe he wouldn't do that naked, but I certainly don't want to know what kind of interrogation tactics Cannon might use.

For the rest of the ride back to my apartment, I stare at my phone and wait for another bubble of text to pop up.

It doesn't.

* * *

TEN HOURS LATER, I'm munching on a Granny Smith apple tart enough to make my eyes water and drumming my fingers on my kitchen counter.

My day off has been a bust.

Cannon hasn't typed a single word on his laptop. The keystroke logger program is alive and well, but there's literally nothing to see.

What if he doesn't use that laptop? I don't know how the hell I'd be able to get a program onto his laptop at the club because there are cameras everywhere.

As soon as the thought hits me, I cringe, and the apple falls to the counter with a bruising thud.

"What if he has cameras in his apartment?" I ask the empty walls surrounding me as my heart rate kicks up eighty-seven notches. "Why didn't I think about that? Shit. Shit. Shit."

I'm not usually such an idiot when it comes to this stuff. The only excuse I have is that Cannon Freeman has thrown me so far off-balance that I don't know what has happened to the normal me who has instincts like a bloodhound.

Backing away from my laptop—where the camera has been covered with a little piece of electrical tape since the day I purchased it—I wonder when all my instincts for self-preservation deserted me.

My best guess? Somewhere between getting jealous that my target was possibly screwing his employees, and my screaming orgasm last night on his desk.

I have to pull it together. I have to ground myself and get back on track.

The best way I know how to do that? Remind myself exactly what the Casso family is capable of.

Pushing away from the kitchen counter, I snag my hot-pink Swiss Army knife out of my purse and head for the bedroom, which only takes four steps in my tiny apartment. Once I've located the flathead screwdriver, I go to work. With a few turns, one screw falls into my hand and the vent swings open, revealing a thick manila folder hidden in the ductwork. Silently, I drop into a cross-legged position on the boring white duvet that matches every other boring white thing in this place, including the boring white nightstand I rest the screw on.

This isn't my real apartment. Just like this isn't my real name.

The only real thing in this place is this folder, containing the pieces of my father's investigation that got him killed.

When I flip open the battered front cover, the first picture that greets me is one of Dominic Casso, except instead of looking like a fierce silver fox, his hair is dark like Cannon's without a single hint of gray. The date on the picture reads February 12, 1994. The collar of Dom's long black overcoat is raised to cover his ears as he walks down the steps of the courthouse.

It was the first of many RICO cases where the charges didn't stick. Teflon Dom isn't his nickname because he likes to cook, after all.

On the back, my dad's handwriting is barely legible, but there's a case number written.

I pulled the records from the court system, but I couldn't figure out what he was after. The charges were all about money laundering, and Dom's lawyer managed to get him off with a jury verdict of *not guilty*.

Could they have bought the jury? It's a possibility, but not something that would be easy to prove.

I turn to the next piece of information in the file, hoping

the time and space since I've sorted through this will allow me to examine it with fresh eyes. Four stapled sheets of lined yellow legal pad slide out next. They're filled with information about all the cases brought against Dom and the prosecutors who failed to gain convictions.

It doesn't matter what the charges were; they've never been able to get him on more than a freaking parking ticket. And even then, there was only one.

Page after page, I leaf through until I see a picture of a man I couldn't identify before, but now I know exactly who he is. Nearly a carbon copy of his son, GTR, who was watching Cannon's apartment this morning, Giancarlo Rossetti also had to have been photographed when he was in his prime.

The rest of the file is filled with photos and notes about incidents that were suspected to be part of the rivalry between the families, but no one has been charged in connection with any of them because there wasn't enough evidence.

"No one who will consent to an interview seems to know the cause of the resurgence of the feud," my father noted, and I can only imagine how much that drove him crazy. *"Other inquiries I've made about the Casso family have been met with suspicion and refusal to speak about anything. Several of my potential sources are either terrified, protecting someone, or both."*

My father was a man who never stopped digging until he felt he'd gotten every possible answer. Then he'd go one step further—review all the unearthed facts as objectively as possible and try to spot the story that no one else could see. That was why Leander Lockwood was incredible at what he did, even before he took the job anchoring the national evening news for two decades. He never stopped investigating. Ever.

"You can't just report what you find on the surface. You always have to go deeper, and when you think you've found everything there is to find, dig another ten feet and then reassess."

That was the secret to his success, and one I've always tried to employ in my own life, even before I was officially employed as an investigative journalist. Nancy Drew had nothing on me, which is why I use names from her stories as my aliases. The fact that no one has caught on yet—that Drew Carson is really just Nancy's father's name, Carson Drew, in reverse seemed quite clever to me.

But I'm less impressed with my cleverness when I look back down at the file and papers spread out before me. *There has to be something here.* I know it.

My gut says that digging into the Casso-Rossetti feud and whatever sparked the resurgence twenty-five years ago is what got my father killed, and I'm not going to stop until I have the answers he wasn't able to find.

Don't worry, Dad. I'm not done digging yet.

A small voice inside me says that he would prefer I burn the file, leave New York, and never come back, but I silence it with a shiver.

CANNON

"*W*hy is this punk-ass piece of shit following me?" I toss my phone on the desk in front of Dom, its screen displaying a grainy photo of Giancarlo Tyrol Rossetti Jr., also known as *GTR*, sitting in his car across the street from my apartment. "And why the fuck does he think he can be this blatant about it?"

Dom leans back in his leather chair and clasps his hands behind his neck. Twin revolvers hang from leather shoulder holsters wrapped around his still-broad shoulders.

"What were you doing that he thought would be interesting to watch?" Dom's raised silver eyebrow punctuates the question he already knows the answer to.

It's on the tip of my tongue to say something crude, like *eating my girl's pussy on my desk while she creamed all over my face*, but the words won't come.

In this family, there's never been much respect for women, but I refuse to drag Drew into that category. She's better than that.

Dom's lips form a smirk when I say nothing. "I guess I can figure that out for myself. I really didn't think you had it in you, Canny Boy. But you manage to surprise me every once in a while. Good for you."

"What's going down with the Rossettis? I thought the truce was solid."

The smirk fades and the old man's gaze sharpens on me. "Since when do you want to know all the details of what's happening in my business? Because last I checked, you've never been involved with anything that required you to get your hands dirty."

He's right. I've lived on the periphery my entire life. Never part of the family, never able to break free from it completely. It's a line that's razor-wire sharp and dangerous as fuck to walk, but it's all I know.

"I've done every damn thing you've ever asked of me since I was fourteen fucking years old." My hands tighten into fists at my sides.

Dom drops his hands to the padded leather arms of the chair and stares me down. "And you'll keep doing every damn thing I ask you to do until the day I meet my Maker or hand over the reins. Won't you, Cannon? Because that's what you do. What everyone tells you to. If you showed even a hint of wanting to take over the family, I would give you a shot. But you don't show me that. You look at everything I've built, with my own fucking bloody hands, with contempt."

My teeth grind together as I force myself to stay silent, even when I want to tell him to go fuck himself, and walk out of this building and this city and never fucking come back. The idea of it—the sheer magnitude of the freedom just beyond my grasp—is seductive as hell.

Start over somewhere else. *Be* someone else.

Why haven't I done it already? I have money Dom knows nothing about. I have real estate he doesn't know I own. Why am I still living under his rule?

Because he's the only family I have left. Despite the fact that I want to hate him . . . I can't. He's still my father, for good or for evil.

"Yeah, that's what I thought. Nothing to say. That's one thing you excel at—keeping your fucking mouth shut. At least until it mattered, and you had to blow shit with Creighton. Lucky for you, he'll still talk to me. Real fucking lucky." Dom rocks back in his chair and crosses his arms over his chest.

"What do you want from me, Dom?" I bite out the question. "I'm running your club. It's making a fuck-ton of money you don't have to clean because I keep it on the up-and-up. Even the Feds aren't watching closely anymore now that I'm in charge. If there's something else you think I should be doing, you just let me know."

I turn to walk out of his office without being dismissed because I just don't give a fuck anymore, about him or getting an explanation about GTR, but Dom stops me as soon as I touch the door handle.

"There is one thing . . ."

I look over my shoulder at him. "What?"

The harsh lines of his face deepen further as he glares at me. "The girl. If you're not fucking her, she's fair game. If last night was a charade, you really won't like the consequences."

With my jaw at risk of cracking, I speak through clenched teeth.

"If you even think about touching her, you'll answer to me. I may not be the son you wanted under your thumb, but I've learned vengeance at your knee. Don't fucking try me, because you'll be meeting your Maker a hell of a lot sooner than you planned."

Instead of rising to his feet and pulling a gun from his

shoulder holster, Dom smirks at me, respect glinting in his eyes.

"Finally. Only took some sweet pussy to make you into a man. Bring her to my birthday party. I want to learn more about Miss Drew Carson."

"*W*hat do you mean, you left him without riding that monster dick all night long after he ate you until you screamed?"

Randi's question comes out like a squeal, and women at the two tables next to us swivel their heads to stare at me like I've betrayed the sisterhood. Thankfully, the rest of the bar is packed, and the noise drowns out her shock before it carries further to elicit more awkward stares.

"Wasn't that enough for one night? Especially *the first night?*" I whisper the question, hoping that the tone of my voice will influence Randi to stop shrieking, but even I know that's a long shot.

Her eyes widen and she shakes her head like she's over-whelmed by the degree of my failure. "No, girl. It's never enough. You should be walking bowlegged right now, because I've heard that man can pound you into the pave-ment without even trying." Randi leans forward, and her boobs threaten to spill free of her low-cut shirt.

I cross my arms and glare at her. "Oh, really? Because the

other stuff you told me—about him fucking all of his employees—wasn't true at all. As a matter of fact, it was the opposite of true. He said he won't touch them."

Instead of being offended by being called out, Randi throws her head back, and her silver-streaked black hair goes flying as she laughs.

"What is so damn funny?"

She wipes her eyes, still chuckling as she reaches for her beer. "I wasn't wrong when it counted. He sure as hell touched *you*, didn't he?"

Goddammit. She's right, and I can't even argue about that.

"But he didn't touch Tanya."

Randi rolls her eyes. "Because Tanya's a bitch who would probably bite a man's dick off if it got too close to her mouth. She's been man-hating since the beginning of time. Besides, I never told you that Cannon fucked her."

A stab of annoyance shoots through me because Randi didn't make any exclusions from the *he fucks everyone, but only one night* speech she gave me before, and she didn't tell me about knowing Tanya. But I let it slide because . . . well, it's Randi. What am I supposed to do with her? She's the closest thing I have to a friend as Drew Carson.

"How do you know Tanya, anyway? And why didn't you tell me you applied there for a job? *Seven times.*"

Randi waves her hand at the waitress, making the universal signal for *we need another round*, which we really don't. I'm already feeling the buzz from drinking after not eating much all day because I was wrapped up in my father's files.

When she's assured the next round is on its way, Randi turns back to me. "Would you advertise you'd been chased away from a place where you wanted a job? Don't judge me.

171

As for Tanya, I met her through Teal, her younger sister. She's a favorite on the party-girl circuit. Guys will buy her *anything*." Randi pulls a twenty out from beneath her bottle of beer. "I swear, she must have a gold-plated pussy, because her blood alcohol level is usually higher than her IQ."

I can picture a younger, less hostile version of Tanya, but the last part makes me wonder if Teal's partying is why she's not working at the club often. It would fit with the question Tanya asked me on my first day about drinking and the warnings she gave me.

"I guess Teal still works at the club, but I haven't met her yet," I say, hoping Randi will keep spilling information.

"She only works there because even Cannon can't bring himself to fire her. Teal says she fucked him, which, for the record," she shoots me a pointed look, "that's why I told you he fucked his employees. That was straight from the ho's mouth, and I had no reason to think she was lying about it."

"He says he didn't," I reply, leaning back in my seat.

Randi's eye roll threatens to pop her eyeballs straight out of her head. "Like any guy ever tells the truth about that shit. That's your first mistake, young Jedi. You believe them. You need to learn to be a little less trusting."

I grab my glass and chug the rest of my dirty martini with one gulp, because I can't school my expression fast enough. If Randi only knew I was the one no one should trust . . . but I can't tell her. Not now and not ever.

When I've regained my composure, I set the glass down and nod. "I'll work on that."

The next round of drinks is delivered, but my phone buzzes incessantly in my purse. I glance inside to see which phone it is—my work phone or my personal phone. Normally, I only bring my work phone with me, but Ariel is due to have a baby at any moment, and I want to know when the screaming bundle of joy makes its arrival into the world.

It's my personal phone. And it's my mother calling. *Great.*

I stand up from the table and point to my phone. "I gotta take this. I'll be right back."

Randi nods, her gaze already wandering to the nearest solo guy in the bar as I walk out to the sidewalk where I'll be able to hear my mother lecture me over God only knows what this time.

Except I'm not quite quick enough.

The ringing dies and I stand on the sidewalk, trying to decide whether I want to call her back. There's no love lost between me and Mom. She bounces from one übertrendy health spa to the next, instead of just checking herself into rehab where she belongs.

Before I make a decision, an alert pops up on the screen indicating I have a new voice mail. Because I'm a glutton for punishment, I tap on it to listen.

"You know you could call me once in a while. I'm not dead like your father."

That's all I need to hear before I hit DELETE. I don't need that kind of negativity in my life—real or fake.

I march back inside the bar, *really* ready for that next drink, and I pause when I see Randi already has a live one on the line.

Dammit.

I take two more steps toward the table when he turns to the side and I catch his profile. *What the hell?*

It's GTR, the guy who was outside Cannon's apartment this morning. *Oh. My. God. That's impossible.* But there's no mistaking that it's him. And he's chatting up Randi like it's his job.

Fucking hell.

What am I supposed to do now? I back away from the direction of the table, slipping behind a tall man, and make a break for the sidewalk. In my haste, I slam into someone and mumble an apology before sprinting to the exit.

Once outside, I text Cannon.

ME: I need you.

32

CANNON

*T*he club isn't as entertaining without Drew here. She's only worked here a few days, and I'm still wishing she didn't have today off.

I've been thinking about Dom's request all day, and how the hell I'm going to get us out of it, but I'm still working out a solution.

My phone vibrates in my suit jacket pocket, and I pull it out to see a text from her. *Like the universe knows I can't get her off my mind.*

But as soon as I read the words, I still. Instead of texting her back, I tap her contact and call. She answers on the first ring.

"What's going on?"

"Well . . . this is going to sound stupid, but I'm out with Randi and I left the table, and when I was going back, that guy who was outside your apartment this morning *was there hitting on her.*"

GTR is in the same bar as Drew?

Fuck. Fuck. Fuck. I should have stayed in Dom's office until I got an answer about GTR or we had a plan to deal

175

with him, but of course I fucking didn't. Now he's getting way too fucking close for comfort.

"Where are you?"

"On the sidewalk out in front of a sports bar called Lambo's."

Thankfully, I know where it is, and it's not that far away. "You sure it's him?" I ask, keeping my tone calm as I grab my keys and gun out of my desk drawer.

"Um . . . dark hair, sideburns that turn into one of those ugly chinstrap lines that's not really a beard."

"Fuck. Stay away from the table. And for God's sake, don't drink anything. I'm on my way." I jam the gun down the back of my suit pants and head out of my office.

"Wait, why?"

"I don't want you even breathing the same air he does, so stay outside. I'm coming." I stride across the club floor, my phone clutched in my hand.

"What about Randi?" Drew's voice rises with concern for her friend. But Randi isn't the one I'm worried about.

"Do what I told you, Drew. Randi will be fine."

"Okay. I'll stay right here, but hurry."

"Good girl." I hang up the phone and hit the entryway where Grice is standing guard.

"Something wrong, Boss?"

"Maybe. I gotta go handle something. Tell Stefano he's in charge of the club floor. I'll call you if I'm not coming back."

My hand is already on the door handle when he asks, "You need backup? Or a piece?"

I shake my head. "I'm strapped. I'll handle it."

"Be safe, Boss."

* * *

IT TAKES me fifteen minutes to get to Lambo's, and a wave of relief washes through me when I see a blonde standing out front.

Thank fuck. She listened.

I hop out of the cab, since it was quicker than calling Warren back from his errand on the other side of town, and head right for her.

Drew looks up from her phone and stills as she spots me.

I don't hesitate for even a second. I stop in front of her, wrap one arm around her, cup her face with my other hand, and kiss the hell out of her. She stiffens at first but relaxes into my hold a second later. I take the kiss deeper, silently telling her I'm so fucking glad she's okay, and finally pull back.

She blinks up at me, her gaze hazier than it was moments before. "What was that for?"

"For this morning," I tell her, but it's a fuck of a lot more than that. I've never had something to lose before. Never had a weakness to be exploited. Now it's clear that the Rossettis have locked onto her as being exactly that. "And because you sounded scared as hell on the phone."

"Why is he here?" she whispers. "Is it a coincidence?"

I shake my head. "No, and we're heading back inside to make sure he understands this shit ain't gonna fly."

Drew's entire body goes tense again. "Are you sure that's a good idea?"

I think of the respect I saw on Dom's face when I threatened him. "Doesn't matter if it's a good idea or not. It's what has to happen. Come on."

I lead Drew back into the packed bar and spot GTR immediately, leaning against a table where Randi Brown sits.

"Has Randi mentioned knowing him? Did she invite him here?" I ask Drew as I glance down at her.

"I don't think she's mentioned him. And she didn't say she was planning on meeting up with anyone. We were just getting together to talk . . . about things."

From the way she trails off after the vague answer, I have a feeling Drew and Randi were getting together to talk about what happened last night between me and the woman who feels perfectly right at my side.

But I couldn't care less about her spilling details, because right now we have a lot more serious concern—why the fuck GTR is following Drew.

As Drew and I walk toward the table, Randi's eyes widen and GTR turns to follow her gaze. When he sees me, there's not even a hint of surprise. A smug smile curls his fucking mouth, and I want to knock his teeth down his throat for it. It's like he wanted me to know that he was following her.

What in the actual fuck?

"You didn't mention your man was coming out tonight," Randi says, sizing me up.

"He surprised me," Drew replies in a light tone. "Randi, you've met Cannon, my—"

"Boyfriend." I finish for her and then spear GTR with a glare. "What the hell are you doing here, Junior?"

He puffs up at the nickname he's been trying to kick since childhood. "None of your goddamned business, Freeman."

"Wait, you two know each other?" Randi looks from me to GTR in shock genuine enough for me to think maybe she doesn't have a clue what kind of scum she's trying to pick up tonight.

"Well enough," GTR says to her before turning to me. "Didn't expect to see you here tonight, though, Cannon. Thought you were working at that fancy club of yours. I think it's about time for me to put in a new membership request. Should get bumped to the top now, yeah?"

He's alluding to the truce that our fathers struck earlier this week, but he should know better than to breathe a word of that shit in a place like this. Then again, GTR has never struck me as intelligent—just brutal.

I curl my arm around Drew's waist and pull her into my side. "Go ahead. Waiting list hasn't gotten any shorter since last time, but you can try."

"You don't want to be a member of that stuffy club," Randi says with a wink at GTR before shooting me a sharp look. "They don't let in women like me."

"Their mistake," GTR says to her. But even with Randi's tits nearly falling out of her shirt, he still cuts his gaze to Drew, and I swear he's one step away from drooling.

Randi doesn't miss his shifting attention as she straightens. "So, what brings you here tonight if you're supposed to be working, Cannon?"

"Couldn't keep my mind on work, so I thought I'd track down my beautiful distraction." I squeeze Drew against my side, making it clear to GTR that she is *off-fucking-limits*.

"Oh my God, that is too freaking precious. Drew, seriously. How did you not fuck this guy?" Randi squeals as she reaches for her drink.

GTR's eyes light up like he's been handed the keys to the kingdom, and I want to strangle Randi Brown. Drew freezes beside me, and I guarantee she's wishing she'd kept her mouth shut.

While I'm working out something to say, Drew presses harder against me.

"Jesus, Randi. You know I'm a fifth-date kind of girl." She glances up at me from under her lashes, and I'm stunned at what a good actress she is. "I did appreciate all the orgasms, though. What do you say we get out of here and have dates two through five all in one night?" Drew bites down on her lip, looking earnest and sexy and innocent all at the same time.

"Well, fuck. Who could turn down that kind of offer," GTR says. "I'd ride her all night—"

I rip my gaze away from Drew's to cut him off. "Shut your fucking mouth and have some goddamned respect. Obviously, your father didn't teach you shit, but you'd think you'd have learned some by now."

His glare is filled with enough acid to strip paint off a car.

"Fuck you, Freeman. You think you're better than me. You and your old man ain't nothing but—" GTR manages to stop himself from saying the one thing that could get him killed faster than anything, talking shit about Dom. He turns and speaks to Randi instead. "What do you say we get out of here, sexy?"

Drew tenses at my side, probably wanting me to stop her friend from going with him, but there's not a damn thing I can do about it. Randi's a grown woman and she doesn't take orders well, which is only one reason I wouldn't hire her.

The woman in question smiles seductively. "I'm going to bang you like a drum, bad boy. I need a little danger to spice up my life. Let's go."

"Randi—" Drew says, but Randi shakes her head.

"You know I'm a first-date kind of girl, and Mama needs to get some tonight." Randi hops off the stool and wraps herself around GTR's side like climbing ivy. "Catch you on the flip side."

The pair walk out of the bar arm in arm, and I lock my fingers around Drew's to keep her from going after them.

"Why did you let her leave with him?" she demands as soon as she cuts her attention from their retreating backs to me, fear for Randi written all over her features. "He's bad, right?"

180

"Which Randi clearly picked up on, and she went anyway. What do you want me to do?"

Drew presses her lips together and doesn't answer right away. In her silence, I look at the abandoned table and the untouched martini sitting on it.

"This yours?" I ask her.

She nods. "Randi ordered another round when I got up to answer my phone. I didn't make it back to the table to drink it."

"And while you were gone, GTR showed up and hit on your friend."

"Yeah, so it seems."

"What kind of drink is this supposed to be?" I pick it up and sniff.

"Dirty martini," she replies as her top teeth bite down on her bottom lip.

The clear liquid has an unusually cloudy appearance, so I take a small sip and a strong, salty flavor hits my tongue.

That motherfucker.

Rage, the likes of which I've never known before, rushes into my bloodstream. Instead of boiling over the way I want to, I force the heat to turn to pure ice. Ice is better because you don't make stupid decisions.

Still, I voice my intent. "I'm going to kill him."

"What?" Drew stares up at me, her eyes wide. "Why?"

"He fucking roofied your drink."

"Then we have to go after Randi. What is he going to do to her?"

My grip on Cannon's hand tightens as I try to drag him away from the table, but he's become an unmovable mountain. Instead of charging after GTR and Randi, he's practically glued to the floor.

"Please," I say, resorting to begging. "We have to do something."

Cannon's expression is as warm as an iceberg when he finally meets my gaze. "Randi will be fine. GTR wouldn't dare hurt her. Not when we watched them leave the bar together. And he's also probably thanking God that we don't know he tried to drug you. But he's fucking wrong about that, and he'll pay with his life."

Suddenly, the man who never seemed to fit the mob profile sounds just like his father. There isn't a single doubt in my mind that he means everything he says.

He plans to kill the heir to the Rossetti crime family, right after they had a secret meeting, for this. For me.

Oh sweet Jesus. What the hell am I supposed to do now?

I have to mitigate the damage. I didn't start this investigation intending to cause a bigger rift between the Rossettis and the Cassos that could easily result in rivers of blood on the streets of New York. While it would solve my problem in a way I didn't consider, I find that I can't stand the thought of Cannon caught in the cross fire.

I have to protect him, even if it's from himself.

Cannon suddenly moves away from the table, and I hurry to fall into step behind him. I don't know where he plans on going, but I don't trust him too far away from me right now, given what just happened.

Instead of leaving, he goes up to the bar, and it's hard to hear him over the conversation and music playing in the background. When the bartender hands him an empty paper coffee cup and lid, things finally click into place in my brain. *He's taking the drink as evidence.* We backtrack to the table, and he dumps the contents of the dirty martini into the cup and snaps the lid on it.

Finally, he turns his attention to me. "Come on. You've got some explaining to do."

"What do you mean?" I blink up at him twice while I try to figure out what the hell kind of information he could possibly want from me.

Without replying, he holds out an arm, indicating that I should precede him out the door. As I move through the thickening crowd, he blocks anyone from getting close to me, but it also makes it impossible to ask any more questions.

When we reach the sidewalk again, I can't help but scan up and down the street, looking for Randi—or Lorenzo, who was following us the night before. Beside me, Cannon is tapping something into his phone, and I assume he's calling for a ride.

Without thinking, I pull out my phone, find Randi's contact, and fire off a text message.

ME: *Please be careful tonight. That guy seemed sketchy AF. Text me when you see this. And when you're home safe and alone. I know you think I'm crazy, but please just do it.*

NOT SURPRISINGLY, Randi doesn't reply immediately, and I don't even want to think about what she's doing instead. *Please stay safe, Randi. I didn't mean to drag you into my mess.* Guilt whips through me, and I try to push it away. *Occupational hazard*, I try to tell myself, but I've never been in a situation like this before.

"Are you sure she's going to be okay?" I ask quietly, watching Cannon's serious face as his attention cuts from his phone to me.

"How many other bad decisions has she made that she's skated away from without any problems?"

It's a valid point, I know, because Randi isn't the most careful with her own personal safety, and that's based solely on what I've learned over the past six months from her.

"A lot."

"Then let's hope her luck holds out for one more."

A knot of tension blooms between my shoulder blades. "I was really hoping for a little more reassurance than that."

Cannon shoves his phone in his pocket and turns to look at me. "GTR isn't stupid enough to hurt her. And don't take this the wrong way . . ." He pauses to glance out at the street and the wailing fire engine that flies by before meeting my gaze again. "But there's no way he's going to throw away a chance at leading the Rossetti family on a piece of ass like Randi."

"What do you mean?" Indignation rises up in me on Randi's behalf, and a chill from the cool air sweeping by us raises goose bumps on my arms.

"Because she's not the same kind of woman you are."

My jaw drops as I try to make sense of what he's saying. "What . . . what do you mean?"

"Randi's one-night material. That's it. He'll get what he wants tonight and move on."

"Then what kind of woman does that make me?" I ask as a shiver works through me.

Cannon yanks one arm and then the other out of his suit jacket. He drapes it over my shoulders. "The kind wars are fought over."

His words wrap around me with more warmth than the jacket, and I know it's dangerous.

While I'm gaping at him, Cannon turns away as the Bentley rolls to a stop in front of the bar. He threads his fingers through mine and pulls me toward the back door.

"Come on. We have a stop to make, and then you and I are going to talk."

CANNON

I shouldn't have said it. Any of it. *Fuck.* I shouldn't have even been at Lambo's tonight, because GTR shouldn't have been there either. But we're all getting fucked up over this woman who has me more off-kilter than anyone I've ever met.

More than anything, I wish I could talk to Creighton about her. I watched him get knocked on his ass by a little powerhouse of a woman who stole his heart before he even realized he had one.

I was so fucking smug and superior about it too. I couldn't figure out why he'd want to disrupt his perfectly ordered life to chase Holly all over the country and make their marriage work. Now I'm starting to get an inkling of why he was willing to drop everything that had always mattered and shift his priorities to accommodate whatever made her happy.

My situation is nothing like his, I remind myself. Creighton is a billionaire who could have anyone and pull any string to make things work. He didn't know he was the bastard son of a mob boss until he was in his thirties, and once he found out, he didn't care. His relationship with Dom hasn't over-shadowed everything in his entire life. He wasn't raised on treachery the likes of which only someone who grew up around the family could understand.

But he's one of the only people on this earth who could possibly have advice for me in this situation . . . and he still won't take my calls.

"Where are we going?" Drew asks, and I put Creighton out of my mind. It's not a problem I can fix right now.

"A friend's—where you'll stay in the car."

"Why?" she asks, her dark brown eyes inquisitive.

I wish she'd quit wearing those contacts. *Not something I'm willing to say in front of Warren, though, because then it would get back to Dom and he'd have way too many questions about it.*

"Because there are certain things you don't need to see."

Twenty minutes later, we pull up in front of a nonde-script brownstone, and I hop out of the car. Ducking my head back inside, I look at Drew.

"I'll be five minutes. Maybe ten. Don't go anywhere."

Her face takes on a mulish expression, but she nods. I glance at Warren, and he smiles.

"We'll be right here, Boss. Take your time."

A feeling of foreboding creeps around the collar of my shirt, but I push it down and jog across the street with the paper coffee cup in hand.

I can practically feel Drew's gaze on my back as I take the steps that lead to the basement unit and knock on the door.

Over the earsplitting sounds of Rage Against the Machine, I wonder if Yoder will be able to hear me.

Shockingly, he yanks the door open a second later. He's got three pairs of glasses on his head, and I don't even want to know why. His gaming headset dangles from one hand.

"Whatchu got for me, man?" he asks, stepping aside for me to enter next to a wobbling tower of empty pizza boxes.

When the door shuts behind me, I hold up the coffee cup.

"Thanks, but you didn't have to do that. I'm already loaded up on caffeine."

"Don't drink this unless you want to wonder what the fuck happened to the last twelve hours of your life when you wake up."

His eyes widen behind the pair of glasses he shoves down onto the bridge of his nose. "Someone tried to roofie you?"

"Not me. A friend."

His mouth forms an O. "Shit. Who the fuck would be that stupid?"

I grit my teeth at the thought of what GTR might have done if Drew hadn't called me. The rage that I turned to ice threatens to burst free in the form of a flow of fucking lava, but I hold it back.

Now isn't the time. Proof first.

"I need you to confirm what was used in the drink. Chemical composition and everything. I want to be able to track it back to the source."

"Ohhh . . . You're getting ready to fuck someone hard, aren't you?"

"I'm just taking out the garbage. We don't need any more assholes running around the city drugging women."

Yoder takes the cup and stares down at it like it contains the secrets of the universe. "I'll do this one for free, man. My sister got date-raped back in college. Seriously fucking uncool."

"Not necessary. I'll take care of you. Get it done as quick as you can, though. I need answers," I say, catching the sound of disembodied players yelling at him through his headset.

Yoder yanks it back up to his ear. "Shit. Sorry. Gotta get

back to my game. I'll get on this as soon as it's wrapped up. I'll text you when it's done."

I know better than to expect a good-bye, because Yoder is already throwing the headset on and talking shit to someone on the other end.

I leave the musty smell of the basement apartment behind and head out to the car, only to see a black-and-white with its flashers on stopped behind the double-parked Bentley.

You've got to be fucking kidding me.

As soon as I step into the street, an unmarked car pulls up behind the squad car, but I know exactly who it is. Detective Clinton Cole, a pain in Dom's ass since the day Cole graduated from the academy.

The fact that he's still alive continues to amaze me, because he's offered up plenty of information to the Feds that helped them bring charges against Dom more than once. Nothing has ever stuck, but Cole hasn't given up.

He's looking for a promotion to detective first grade, but he won't get it until he makes a major bust. Which, no doubt, he's looking for the Casso family to provide. The only problem—he's never come sniffing around me before. I've always skated by with my connections to Creighton Karas, but after I left Karas International, my veneer of respectability has grown thin.

Cole spots me as soon as I hit the pavement and lifts his chin in my direction. "Mr. Freeman, what brings you to Mr. Yoder's this evening?"

"Detective Cole, what a surprise to see you here." I don't even bother to look at the uniformed officer standing by the Bentley, no doubt asking for Warren's license and registration. "Something I can help you with?"

He shrugs nonchalantly, but I can read between the lines. This is no accident. "I heard there was a fancy Bentley double-parked in this neighborhood and thought I'd swing by and see what you were doing. Didn't plan on staying long?"

Inside the car, Drew is cringing into the corner of the back seat, her hair sweeping down into her face.

"Only long enough to drop off some coffee," I say, but Cole doesn't buy it.

"Seems awfully nice of you, and I know you're not that nice of a guy."

I smile at the detective. "You know that's not true, Cole. Even if I did leave you off my Christmas card list last year."

"Who's your friend?" Cole tilts his head to look into the back seat of the car from the open front window.

"An employee who needed a ride."

He ducks down to get a closer look, and I want to rip him away from the car. "What's her name?"

"My employee. That's all that matters." I give the answers through clenched teeth, hanging on to my pretense of politeness by a thread. I'm hoping Drew picks up on my cues to stay silent and let me do the talking.

"Hey, miss. You okay back there?"

From around Cole's head, I get a better view of her as she lifts her chin to look at him.

"I'm fine, thank you," she says.

Cole's posture stiffens. "Have we met before? What's your name?"

Drew shakes her head. "Sorry, I never forget a face, and I don't recall yours."

"Huh. Must be my mistake." He rises to his full height and shoves his hands in his pockets. "What the hell are you doing mixed up with family business, Freeman? I thought you knew better than to get your hands dirty."

"Your concern is admirable, Detective, but I don't know

what you're talking about. I manage one of the city's oldest private clubs, and we have to suspend taking membership applications when the waiting list hits thirty years long."

His sharp gray gaze doesn't buy my spiel, and I'm not surprised. Cole isn't stupid, and in another life, he's the kind of guy I might have grabbed a beer and watched a game with. But that's not the world I live in.

"You can hold the party line all you want, but when I bring down Dom, you're going with him if there's even a shred of evidence that connects you to all the shit he's buried. No one stays on top forever."

"Thanks for the warning. Have a good night, Detective."

Cole's gaze slips to the window Warren rolls up as the officer walks back to his car. Part of me says he's looking for another glimpse of Drew, and I want to know why. "You too, Freeman. You too."

Once Cole has walked back to his unmarked car, I slip into the back seat of the Bentley and turn to Drew.

"Do you know him?"

3 5

D R E W

uck. Fuck. Fuck.

Clinton Cole's presence is an unexpected surprise. And by surprise, I mean those bad ones, like when you're standing on the corner hailing a cab and nearly get creamed by a bus swerving to miss a jaywalker.

Now Cannon's staring at me, and his question hangs in the air between us like a floating guillotine blade.

"Know the cop?" I shake my head and feign surprise at the question, even while I hate myself for lying. "Like you, I try to avoid them."

"Why did he think he recognized you?"

"No idea. I just have a familiar face. People mistake me for someone else all the time."

Cannon's gaze narrows. "Is that why you wear the wig and contacts? To blend in? You don't want to stand out?"

A million more lies are on the tip of my tongue, but they won't come out. Instead, a portion of the truth falls from my lips.

"You're right. I don't want people to remember me. It creates too many complications. Please don't ask me why." I don't know why I tack on that last part, because it's just going to make him ask more questions.

But I overheard what Cole said to him—that when Dom goes down, Cannon's going with him if there's even a shred of evidence that implicates him in Dom's business.

That was the exact same attitude I had before, but now I want the opposite. I need to prove that Cannon has nothing to do with the Casso family's illegal enterprises, because I couldn't live with myself if my duplicity ruined his life.

Beside me, Cannon's chest rises and falls slowly as he stares straight ahead. I would give anything to know what's going through his mind right now, because I'm only a hair's breadth away from blowing my cover completely. If he asks me another question, I won't be able to lie to him again. I'll tell him everything. The complete truth.

I glance at Warren in the front seat and hope like hell he's trustworthy, because this could cost me *everything.* Including my life.

When Cannon opens his mouth, I'm already preparing myself, but what he says shocks me.

"Take Ms. Carson and me back to my apartment, Warren. I'm not returning to the club."

I turn and look at him, wondering again what's going through his brain, but this time, I'd give just about every penny I have to my name to find out.

For most of the ride, weighty silence dominates the cabin of the car. Cannon says nothing else about Cole or the person with whom he left the drink. I want to ask a dozen questions, but since I don't want to answer any in front of Warren, I keep quiet.

I'll have time tonight . . . although, I'm really hoping interrogation isn't on the menu, because I can think of a lot of other things I'd rather do with the man beside me.

Gah. I'm not supposed to feel like this. I had no idea that the myriad pitfalls I would encounter during this investigation would include being so attracted to my target that I can't even think straight half the time.

My phone buzzes in my purse, thankfully distracting me from my thoughts, and I carefully fish it out to see the screen. *Mom.*

Shit.

For the second time tonight, I wish I'd just left this damn phone at my apartment like I usually do. Regardless, I definitely can't answer this call here.

Cannon glances over at me and down at the phone before I can tuck it away again. "You're not going to answer?"

Shaking my head, I quickly hide the screen before shoving it back in my bag. "It's no big deal. My mom."

"Moms are important."

"You've never met mine. She'll talk for an hour, and I won't be able to get a word in edgewise, even to tell her it's not a good time. And that's including all the questions she'll ask that she won't give me time to answer."

When he nods slowly, I can't help but wonder if he's thinking about his mom, and my heart breaks for the way he lost her. Even though he hasn't told me himself, I know the details from the news articles about her death that were in my father's file. No one should ever have to go through that. I can relate because I feel the same way about my dad.

As Cannon continues to stare at me, the awkward silence closes in, so I start babbling things I should keep to myself because they're the *truth*. "She's a piece of work. Divorced my dad when I was fourteen because she wasn't the center of his life. She was jealous of his work and hated coming second to anything. She constantly accused him of sleeping with coworkers."

"Did he?" Cannon asks carefully.

I pause to flip through my memory of all the people I met at the networks as a kid. "Not that I know of, but I guess it's possible. He was human and fallible, but I like to think he was faithful to her, even though she was awful, especially as the divorce dragged out for almost two years. She fought tooth and nail for every penny she could get, while making it clear she never needed to see me again if he gave her the money."

I slip my fingers into Cannon's, needing the contact.

"Damn, that's hard on a kid," he says, lifting our joined hands to his mouth to press a kiss to my knuckles. "I'm sorry you went through that."

"It probably wasn't as hard as it should have been. I wanted them to split up. I hated living in a house that felt like a war zone, even if the war mostly came from one side of the battle lines in every passive-aggressive way you could imagine. Walking on eggshells got old, really fast."

We reach a blocked intersection, and Warren slows down behind the honking cars.

"So you lived with your dad after?" Cannon asks.

"As much as I could. He worked a lot but had an awesome housekeeper who would keep me company if my mom was out of town on the rare weekends when I was supposed to be with her."

I squeeze his hand as a pang of loss sweeps through me when I think of Antonia. She retired from working for my father when I was twenty and in college, and moved in with her daughter. She died a few years later from complications with pneumonia. My mother had said she probably did it to herself by living an unhealthy lifestyle.

My knuckles turn white as my hands fist at the memory. *Of course, everything that happens to someone else is because of something* they *did, but when it comes to her, it's always someone else's fault.* The double standard is maddening, but I've learned not to get worked up by it. Why I am now, I don't know. Probably too many emotions running high.

Thankfully, Cannon interrupts the downward spiral of my thoughts, saying, "You grew up with money."

Immediately, I wonder if I've said too much. Actually, there's no wondering about it, because I shouldn't have told him any of it. I've never had this problem when going undercover before, but Cannon changed everything. I pull myself back and focus on answering honestly, but not in too much detail.

"My dad did well," I reply, and then the acid from memories of my mom pours in. "And my mom had no problem demanding more alimony every single year that he did better."

"She didn't work?" Cannon tilts his head to the side to study me as I loosen my grip on him.

I choke on a laugh. "No. Never. She would even tell you she was meant to be a trophy wife."

His chest rises with an answering chuckle, but it sounds more forced than humorous. "And did she end up being a trophy wife for someone else after your dad?"

"Oh, definitely not. Because then she would've had to give up the alimony he paid her." We turn a corner sharply to make a light, and I lean into Cannon's solid shoulder.

"Ah. One of those."

"Yep," I say, letting the *p* pop from my lips. "She's definitely one of those."

"Where does she live now?" His voice is back to being whiskey smooth, instead of charged with anger like when we pulled away from the curb.

"California," I say, keeping it vague just in case, because

Lord knows she wouldn't be that hard to track down in San Diego. "She hates any place that doesn't have perfect weather for her to show off her bikini body."

We're closing in on his apartment building, which has my senses heightening. I'm answering way too many of Cannon's questions. I need to get the hell out of the car—and fast—so I can pull myself together, or else I'm going to spill everything.

Hell, that's probably what's going to happen anyway as soon as I get inside his loft.

Am I ready for that? Yes. God, yes. But also—*hell no.* Can I trust him? Truly trust him?

I want to. More than anything. But I definitely don't trust Warren, and before my honesty streak gets wider, we need to get away from him.

As soon as the Bentley glides to a stop, I grab the handle and yank it, shoving the door open as quickly as I can. The suit jacket slips off my shoulders and pools into a puddle on the floorboard of the car.

"*Shit.* I'm so sorry. I didn't mean to throw your jacket—"

Cannon's presence warms me from behind as he cups my elbows with both hands. "In a hurry to get up to my place, Drew?"

Chills ripple over my skin at his nearness, and I want to soak up the feeling, but hearing my fake name on his lips steals any intimacy of it.

I want to tell him. I need to tell him. But not here.

"Just need some fresh air." Turning to look over my shoulder, I ask, "Are you sure you don't need to go back to the club?" I reach for the jacket, but Cannon releases one of my elbows and snags it first with his free hand.

"I'm sure. Trust me."

My stomach flips at his words as he turns me in his arms

until we're almost pressed together. His warm gaze searches my face for answers I can't give him. *God, I want to trust him.* But would it be the worst mistake of my life?

Instead of chancing it, I change the subject the best way I know how. I lean toward him and plant my lips on his.

Cannon doesn't even flinch in surprise. No, he wraps an arm tighter around me and pulls me closer into his body, taking the kiss deeper and hotter.

When he releases me, I wobble on the heels of my shoes. "Jesus, how do you do that to me?"

A glint shimmers in his ever-changing eyes. "I don't know, but I want to do it again."

With one hand on my elbow, he leads me across the street to his building. His hand grips mine like I'm a lifeline, or like he's afraid I'm going to disappear at any moment.

Which I could. And should.

I'm in too deep. I want things I shouldn't want. *But I can't walk away from this. Or from him.* It's a conundrum of epic proportions, and a situation I've never found myself in.

Before I can make sense of the mess that's my brain, a short, stout gray-haired man pops out of the pizza shop, calling Cannon's name.

"Hey, Geno. They get your oven fixed?" Cannon asks, walking back toward the storefront of the building.

"Yeah, yeah. I can't thank you enough for calling in a favor to get them out here the same day. I would've been screwed without you." The old man walks toward Cannon, extending his arm to shake hands.

"No problem at all," Cannon replies, wrapping him in a half hug. "They do work at the club all the time. And it's the least they could do to make sure New York is properly fed and doesn't miss a day of your food."

Cannon's manner with the old man tells me they've been

friends for a while. Calling in favors to get his oven fixed? Yeah, that's exactly what Cannon would do. It reminds me that he said the reason he bought the building was to keep Geno from getting evicted.

He can't possibly be doing bad things, right? But even I'm not so naive to believe that life is black and white. We're all living in the shades of gray, especially me.

"And who is this stunner on your arm? I don't believe I've met her before. An oversight, I'm sure," Geno says with a grin aimed in my direction, his New York accent growing thicker to overshadow the Italian.

Cannon glances down at me with a smile before introducing me to Geno. "This is Drew. I haven't introduced her to your pizza yet. Definitely an oversight."

Geno lights up. "Then tonight is her lucky night. I'm going to make you a feast. Antipasto, calamari, manicotti, pizza, and a little tiramisu to top it off."

I blink at the man as he punctuates the end of his sentence with a clap of his hands. "Wow. That sounds incredible."

"Geno's is more than pizza. But only for my special customers do I break out the manicotti and the antipasto."

"Don't let Mr. Steal Your Girl lie to you," Cannon says with a laugh. "They're on the menu every day."

Geno winks at him. "You know when I make them for pretty girls, I do an even better job. Give me twenty minutes, tops. Then you can come down and bring it up to her. Keep your clothes on until then. She's too skinny. She needs food before . . . you know."

A hot flush burns up my chest because . . . well, it's not every day that an older Italian-American man talks about you having dinner before you get down and dirty with the guy you're not even supposed to be entertaining naked thoughts about.

But now that's all I'm doing.

I can't even make any promises that I'll last twenty minutes, not once I see the couch where I got my hands on Cannon's beautiful cock.

"I'll be down, G. And you mind your own business, old man."

Geno throws his head back, and his thick gray eyebrows wiggle as he laughs. "Get out of here, kid. I gotta cook."

We walk back around to the side door of the building, and Cannon unlocks it to let me in first. Once we're up the elevator and in his apartment, he turns to me.

"I hope you're hungry, because whatever Geno says he's making, count on it being double. And it's damn good."

"He's really sweet. You can tell he cares about you."

With a shrug, Cannon hangs his keys on a hook in his kitchen as I slip off my shoes. "I did what anyone would do. Geno's a good man, and that business is his legacy."

I give him a sideways look as I move across the space to settle myself on a bar stool to avoid looking at the couch. "I can't think of anyone else who would buy a building *in New York* to save an Italian restaurant from foreclosure."

He moves to a cupboard and pulls out a bottle of wine. "I like Geno. We lived in the building across the street when I was a kid. He always made sure there was a slice of pizza for me when I was hungry after school, or when my mom would . . ."

Cannon trails off, and I'm grateful he's shared even this much with me. It's not hard to imagine a little dark-haired boy rushing across the street for a steaming-hot piece of pizza after school.

"You don't have to tell me, but I'd love to hear your story,"

I tell him. It's the most honest thing I can say. I want to learn everything about Cannon. I want to know what made him into the man he is today. What his life was like before. What makes him tick.

Reaching into another cabinet, he pulls out balloon wineglasses and sets them on the counter in front of me. For a moment, I think he's ignoring what I said, but he eventually starts to speak again.

"My mom wasn't cut out to be Dom's mistress. She was meant to be someone's wife." He sucks in a deep breath, and his wide chest rises and falls. "She was sweet. Wanted to make someone's life just as sweet as she was."

"How did she . . . how did she end up with . . ." I can't quite get the question out, but Cannon doesn't need to hear the rest of it.

"She was at the opera one night. Saved for months to buy the ticket, and made the dress with material she got for free from the fabric store she worked at. She was starstruck by the people, and then by the performance." Cannon rounds the counter and hops up on top of it beside me. "Ma said she didn't even care that she was in the nosebleed seats and could barely see, because it was the most beautiful thing she'd ever heard in her life."

I lean into the heat of his body beside me as I picture a woman with Cannon's coloring and hazel eyes, gazing down at the stage as the actors sang in Italian. "That sounds like an incredible night for her."

He gives me a short nod as he reaches for the corkscrew. "Should've been. But she just had to get up at intermission and splurge on a glass of champagne. That's when she met him."

"It's hard to picture Dom at the opera. It doesn't seem like it'd be his thing." I know I'm making a broad generalization, but it's still true.

"Dom hates the opera, but his wife loved it," Cannon replies, his tone taking on a sharp edge.

His wife. In all my research and digging, I've found very little about Lorena Casso. She was mentioned briefly here and there, but there was nothing in depth. Her family history was difficult to track as well. She was raised in a small village in Italy, and from what I could tell, she was shipped over to the US just in time to meet her husband the week before her wedding day.

"How did he meet your mother if he was there with his wife?" I ask quietly.

"Hell if I know. He should've stayed in his damn box, where they'd be waited on hand and foot. But something was different that night. The way she told it, crowds parted for Dom like he was a king. Back then, he was rising to power in a very decisive fashion, so it's not hard to imagine."

He pours the red into both glasses and hands one to me before continuing.

"Of course, a girl from Brooklyn would be stunned to see a man like Dom and the respect he commanded. And with his eye for beautiful women, Dom couldn't miss her. Even in her homemade dress and cheap shoes, he knew she was special."

Cannon sounds equal parts sad and angry right now. I want to tell him it's okay, that he doesn't have to tell me anything more, but I can't bring myself to speak. The faraway look in his eye tells me that he's slipped into the story his mother used to tell and isn't ready to leave it.

"Then what happened?" I ask, reaching up to adjust my wig, wishing I could rip the dang thing off while he's baring his soul.

"He insisted on buying her that glass of champagne and then charmed the hell out of her. Found out where she worked. Promised he'd come see her, and they'd have champagne together. Talked to her until the lights flashed and he had to get back to his box. She watched the rest of the opera with one eye, looking for him with the other, but she couldn't find him. Probably because she didn't have those little opera glasses to snoop on people like everyone else. She thought she'd never see him again, and by the time she made it home to Brooklyn, she said she'd put him out of her mind."

"But Dom didn't forget her, did he?"

Cannon's head moves slowly from side to side while I lift my glass to my lips.

"No. He found her on Monday at the fabric shop. Took her to lunch. Made her feel beautiful. And then he came back every single day and took her to eat until she finally couldn't resist him." He pauses, the muscle in his jaw ticking. "She'd tell the story to me at bedtime like it was a fairy tale. She just didn't realize it would end in a nightmare. She didn't realize he was married; she always made sure to tell me that. She never would've gotten involved with a married man if she'd known."

He flattens one hand on the counter, around the base of his glass, and I cover it with mine.

Cannon keeps speaking without acknowledging my touch. "It's hard to condemn her for it, because I wouldn't be alive if she hadn't met him, but . . ." He glances up at me, his features tight. "Fuck. I didn't mean to get into something this heavy right now."

"You don't have to say anything else. It's fine."

Cannon shakes his head again, moving his hand so he can squeeze mine. As he does, he says, "I can't help but wonder if she'd still be alive if I'd never been born."

My heart breaks for him. Right then. Right there.

"I am so sorry, Cannon. It wasn't your fault. Wondering things like that will never bring you any peace. Trust me, I wonder all the time if my father would still be alive if I'd done something different to trip the wheels of fate and send them rolling in another direction."

My voice grows husky as the words choke me up. And then there's the thought blaring through my brain right now —one I can't tell Cannon.

Did my father have to die for me to meet this man? The one I'm falling in love with?

I have to tell him the truth. Right now.

"There's something I need to—" I say, but a buzzer sounds from the area near the door.

Cannon's gaze lifts to meet mine. "That's Geno. Always quicker than he says. I'll run down and get the food. Drink your wine. No more heavy shit tonight. Just . . . us. Okay?"

He releases my hand and slips away, giving me a reprieve that I don't even want.

CANNON

I know she's going to tell me something I don't want to hear. Something that's going to change everything. If I were a smart man, I'd drag every bit of information out of this cagey woman I can get, but tonight, I don't want to be smart.

No. Tonight, I just want her.

Reckless as fuck, but I don't care. Sometimes you have to take risks. Leaps of faith. That's what the hell I'm doing right now.

Telling Drew my mother's story reminds me that there's not a damn thing we can do to change the path of fate. Drew came into my life for a reason, and I'm not ready to find out exactly what that reason is. Tonight, I just want to pretend that we're two people who want to be with each other, and if we're lucky, we'll both be able to silence the ghosts that haunt us.

When I come back upstairs with a giant pizza box and two huge bags of food, loaded down with what Geno called *all the necessities for seduction*, Drew hasn't moved. She's still at the counter, sipping her wine and watching the door.

As soon as I enter, she pops out of her seat and rushes over to help, but I shake my head.

"I've got it. I promise I can carry Italian food safely. I wouldn't dare commit the cardinal sin of dropping it."

The smile that lifts the corners of her mouth is too fucking beautiful for words. It gives me all sorts of ideas about where tonight is going, and every single one of them is going to be fucking amazing.

I haven't felt this way about a woman in years. Maybe ever.

Something about Drew Carson is different, and if I were fatalistic enough to believe like my mother, I'd say the universe sent her to me for a reason.

"At least let me take the box, and not just because I want to steal a slice. God, this smells *amazing*."

"Geno knows his shit. He's been cooking since he was eight years old, if you believe his stories, which I do," I tell Drew as I settle the bags on the counter.

"That's pretty impressive," she says.

"Yeah, but he's not the best businessman, which is why he got into trouble with his former landlord."

"How long ago did you buy the building?"

"This one? About eight years ago, when I was . . ." I pause, not sure if I want to talk about Creighton and why I no longer work for him.

"You were . . ." Drew prompts me as she glances up from the dozen containers now lining the counter.

"I was working for Creighton Karas."

She presses her lips together for a beat before speaking. "You mentioned that. How'd you go from working for him to running the club?"

I unearth plates and plasticware from Geno's bags and set them on the counter in front of two stools before meeting her gaze and deciding to take a risk. Whatever she does with the information is going to tell me more than my gut will.

"I got fired for feeding information to Dom."

This time, Drew's eyes go wide. "What?"

"Creighton and I are half brothers, except he didn't know it and I did. Dom sent me to school to make friends with him. Become his right-hand man. As long as I reported back to Dom about everything, I had it made. Easy street."

"What happened?" Drew looks up from opening a container of manicotti.

I meet her brown gaze and wish I could see the true color. "Eventually, I got sick of lying to someone I cared about." The statement is pointed as hell, and if I'm wrong, I'll apologize to her. Then I remember that I said *no more heavy shit tonight*, and that's exactly what I'm doing. "Anyway, it's all in the past. Let's eat. I promise this is some of the best Italian you'll have in the city. Maybe the planet."

I grab the bottle of wine to refill her glass. Drew is silent beside me, but I swear to Christ I can feel her open her mouth again and again, as though she wants to speak but can't bring herself to do it.

At least knowing she wants to tell me why she's lying to me is something.

Maybe I am just like my mom. Willing to settle for scraps.

The thought sends a bolt of anger through me.

No. No, I will not fucking settle for scraps. But I will take my time finding out what I need to know. Drew Carson is going to come clean and tell me all her secrets. She will.

Because deep down, I want to believe she's battling the same demons I was with Creighton—fighting the lies and wanting to tell the truth even more.

"*D*id Geno think I was secretly a competitive eater, because holy crap, we barely put a dent in what he sent up," I say thirty minutes later as I stare at the massive amount of food still left between us. *How did Geno think we could possibly eat all of it?*

Cannon smiles, and it's much more lighthearted than the serious expression he had on his face when he went down to get the food. True to his word, he changed the subject to funny stories about living in New York and the crazy things he's seen over the years that make him think nothing could shock him anymore.

"Geno wants to fatten everyone up. He doesn't trust skinny people." Cannon points at me with the end of a half-eaten breadstick.

I give Cannon and his physique a sidelong glance. "I hate to break it to you and Geno, but you're not fat or skinny. You're fit as hell."

Heat kicks up in Cannon's gaze. "You've been checking out my ass, haven't you? I knew I felt something back there."

"So what if I was? It was only fitting with how much you checked out mine."

Now his grin grows. "Damn right, and yours is perfect. I've been dying to get you naked and in my bed."

A punch of lust shoots through me, and there's nothing I want more right now than this man. I glance over my shoulder toward the bedroom and then back at Cannon.

"Is that your version of an invitation? Because I thought you were way smoother than that."

A languid and decadent expression overtakes his face. "With you, I don't want to be smooth. I just want to be me."

Oh God. His words hit me like nothing else could, shaking me to the very foundation of my soul. I want to give him the same. Me, and nothing else.

And I can. No lies. Just me.

"Give me five minutes." I hop off the stool, grab my purse, and rush into the bathroom before he can say anything.

Inside, I stare at my reflection as I pull off the wig, comb out my hair, and remove my contacts. If I had face wash, I'd wash off all the makeup too, but I don't. This will have to be good enough.

My intentions are as pure as they've ever been in my life.

I don't want to hide behind my disguise anymore. I want to give him *me*, which is something I've never given anyone before. Ever.

When I step out of the bathroom, Cannon shuts the door of the fridge and turns to face me. The wine is still on the counter, but the remains of the dinner and the leftovers that could feed two people for a week are gone.

When he sees me, he doesn't hesitate. He stalks across his kitchen and stops with not even an inch between us.

"You're so fucking beautiful, Dr—"

I plaster my lips to his before he can say my phony name.

209

I don't want to hear it on his lips. I want to hear *my name* in that deep, smooth voice, and I promise myself that'll be next. Tomorrow. Soon.

Cannon wraps the fingers of his free hand around the back of my neck, taking the kiss deeper as his tongue strokes mine. When he pulls back to stare into my eyes, it's only to murmur, "God, I want you."

"Good, because I don't think I can stand waiting another minute for this."

Cannon sets me away from him a few inches. His hazel eyes scan up and down my body, as if taking in every detail, before he lunges forward to sweep me off my feet. Literally.

With his mouth on my neck, he carries me into his bedroom and lowers me slowly onto the jade-green duvet covering the king-size mattress. His lips glide along my chin and then back down my neck, pressing kiss after kiss to every part of me I never knew was this sensitive. My ear, my jaw, the curve of my shoulder. And as he does it, his clever hands strip me until I'm in my bra and panties. Only then does he pause to look down at me like I'm his reward for a lifetime of good deeds.

"You're so fucking perfect." His hazel gaze roams over my body, and I reach up to slide a finger between the buttons of his shirt and tug him down to me.

"I want to see you too."

With a grin curving his lips, he reaches for the buttons. In less time than I would have thought possible, he strips out of his jacket and shirt before going for his belt.

My fingers collide with his as I try to help, reaching down between our bodies. In my eagerness, I probably slow him down, but I don't care. I'm a full and willing participant in this, and I want him just as badly as he wants me.

When his cock springs into my hand, I wrap my palm around it and squeeze.

The harsh sigh that escapes his lungs makes me bolder and even more confident. I scoot sideways and change positions so I can guide him toward my mouth. The molten need burning in his gaze tells me that he wants it, even if he won't ask. *Yet.*

I don't know why, but I have the sense that Cannon Freeman is holding back right now because he doesn't want to overwhelm me.

That's just more for me to discover later.

I lap at the head with my tongue, reveling in the strangled groan released from his lungs. After I've finally taken him deep and established a rhythm, he pulls away, his hands locked around my shoulders.

"No more. I'm not coming in your mouth. Not right now."

That's when he starts flexing his dominant streak.

Cannon reaches for me, and a second later, my ass is perched on the edge of the bed, and he drops to his knees in front of me, pulling my panties aside to *feast*. Last time, he started slow and worked up to full strength, but not now. He's a man on a mission, and that mission is my orgasm.

I'm hanging on by a thread when he bites down just hard enough on my clit to send me screaming over the edge.

Only then does he pull away and yank open the nightstand drawer. I watch as he tears open the foil packet and then rolls the condom down his shaft, wishing it was my mouth doing the honors.

Except, if it were, I would have missed the way Cannon grips his cock and strokes, handling himself roughly. There's something so ridiculously hot and masculine about it, another wave of wetness floods my center. I'm dying for him. I need him inside me.

"Hurry." It's the only word I can manage to get out, and instead of following my order, Cannon smiles.

"Oh, baby, there's one thing I'm sure as hell not going to do with you, and that's hurry."

Cue melting into the bed, because the look on his face is pure appreciation. I've never been one of those women who walks around with massive amounts of body confidence, but I do try to appreciate what I've been given. I'm not perfect. I have love handles and cellulite and always seem to be five pounds or more from my goal weight, but in this moment, I'm nothing but grateful. The way Cannon stares at me . . . it's like I'm a goddess and he's never seen anything as beautiful as me, lying before him, waiting to welcome him inside me.

And maybe I am. I arch my back as he comes toward me, and my hands reach for the clasp on my bra and toss it aside.

Cannon releases the grip on himself to snag the waistband of my panties between two hooked fingers. One corner of his mouth quirks up as he says, "Sorry."

I open my mouth to ask why, but before the words are out, the elastic snaps. *Holy hell.* The heat in his gaze as he tosses the ruined underwear aside makes all the difference in the world.

"Please."

"I plan on pleasing you."

In any other moment, his line might be cheesy, but as he steps between my legs, bending over me to drag his lips across the slope of my breast, to capture my nipple in his mouth and give it a nip and a tug, it makes me even more desperate for him.

"I've wanted you like this since the moment you walked

into the club." His voice comes out as a growl as he nudges the head of his cock against my entrance and his eyes narrow. "Do you know how frustrating it is to want someone so badly and know you can't have her? It drove me absolutely fucking nuts."

I reach out to skim the hard muscles of his thighs with my fingertips, urging him forward and wishing I could curl my palms around the perfect curve of his ass.

"There's nothing stopping you from having me now," I whisper, because it's the absolute truth.

But for some reason, his gaze darkens. "There are a million things that should stop me, but not a goddamned one will. I staked my claim. I meant it. You are *mine*." On the last word, he plunges into me, balls deep, with a single stroke.

My breath gets caught in my throat and a moan comes out a garbled cry. My back arches, as if I'm lifting my hips in homage to him. Cannon reaches beneath me and grips my ass, raising me higher, so he can pull out almost completely. With just the head of his cock inside me, he stares into my eyes and repeats it again.

"Mine. All fucking mine." He tunnels inside me again and again, and with every stroke, he brushes against my G-spot, lighting me up until I'm begging for release.

"Please. Please."

From beneath my heavy lids, I watch as a devastating smile sneaks onto Cannon's face. Self-satisfied and confident, he grips my hips and fucks me exactly the way he wants. As I thrash and grip the sheets for stability, he moves his thumb, sweeping it over my clit.

It's like someone found the button for demolition, because that's exactly what he does to me—destroys every single barrier left between us.

"Cannon!" I scream his name as I'm torn away from my

hold on reality and plunged into pleasure, where sparks burst in my field of vision.

Even then, he doesn't stop. He fucks into me harder and faster, his thumb increasing its pressure until I can't say a single intelligible word. All I am is sensation and need and desperation.

"Again. Give it to me again." He grunts out the order, and I can do nothing but whip my head from side to side.

On the edge of a ragged breath, I manage to get out a muddled reply. "Can't. Too much."

He releases his hold on my ass to lean forward and press his forehead to mine for a second. "No. You can take it. Take more. Own it, baby. It's fucking yours." He presses a kiss to my lips. "Just like I am. Take me. All of me."

I blink and his close-up features turn hazy, but I see everything I need to see. His eyes are clear and filled with desire for *me*.

"Whatever you want," I mumble. "Anything."

"That's my girl. Now fucking come for me."

He pulls back and unleashes one last torrent of powerful strokes that ignite every nerve ending in my body.

"Ahhh! Oh my God—Cannon!" My cry echoes off the high ceilings, enveloping us both as I lose myself into the unbelievable rush of sensations. My heart hammering, legs shaking, I come harder than I've ever come in my life.

Through the static in my ears, I hear Cannon roar one word.

"Mine!"

38

CANNON

*H*er head lolls to one side as I brace myself over her body, beads of sweat rolling down my chest. My heart threatens to explode, but I can't stop. Won't stop. Not until she understands, in the best way I can tell her, that this isn't a game anymore. This isn't us putting on a show to keep her safe from Dom.

This is *us*. Me and the most fascinating woman I've ever met. The woman who might just have ruined me for all others. But at least, if I'm lucky, I've done the same for her.

She's mine.

That's nonnegotiable.

I may not know every goddamned thing about her, but I know enough to make my decision. Everything else comes second to following my instincts, and they laid claim to her the moment she walked through the door.

I tried to resist it. Push it away. Tell myself she was off-limits, but I should have known I couldn't fight it.

Dipping my head from where it hangs above her chest, I press a kiss to her jaw. "I'll get you a washcloth, baby. Stay right here."

I start to pull out, but her limp hand lifts off the covers and grips my forearm. "Not yet. Please. Just . . . stay a second."

I drop another kiss at the corner of her mouth. "You like being full of me?"

Her hips shift, and she presses me back inside.

"I'll take that as a yes."

Finally, her eyes open, and those piercing turquoise-blue irises stare back at me. "You can take that as a hell yes." Then her lids drift closed, and I know she's moments away from dropping off into an exhausted sleep.

I can handle that.

After another thirty seconds, I pull out and she doesn't protest. Her chest rises and falls in a steady rhythm. *Asleep.*

I can't help the smile that tugs at the corners of my mouth as I glance in the bathroom mirror and then dispose of the condom.

"She's the one," I whisper to no one in particular, but that's because the words are for someone very specific—my mother.

She told me I'd know, without a shadow of a doubt, when I met *her*. I never believed my overly romantic mother because I chalked up the sentiment to her being too young when Dom swept her off her feet. At least, I didn't believe her until this very moment. I've stayed alive by following my gut, and it's never led me astray, so I have to believe it now.

She's the one. This is it.

After wetting a washcloth with warm water, I move quietly back into the bedroom where Drew is still sleeping. She's out, not even waking up when I gently clean her up and then move her onto a pillow. Once she's tucked beneath the sheet and comforter, I press a kiss to her forehead.

"Sleep, baby. I'll be right here."

Except, I didn't know that I was lying.

As soon as I move out into the kitchen to grab a leftover slice of pizza to feed my growling stomach, I see my phone on the counter. The screen is lit up with notifications. Texts and calls. All from employees at the club.

Well, fuck.

I take a bite and call Grice, because he's the most likely to give me an unbiased rundown of whatever the hell is going on to precipitate this many calls.

Visions of flames licking up the building dance in my head until he picks up.

"What's going on? Is everyone okay?"

"Thank fuck, you finally called. What do you want me to do with her?" His question makes no sense because I have absolutely no context at all.

"Who? What happened?" I ask, then choke down the bite of pizza.

"Teal. Stefano posted the schedule for next month, and when she saw she wasn't on it, she flipped the fuck out. I thought she knew she was done. Didn't you tell her, Boss?" Grice's frantic tone tells me what I've long suspected—that his soft spot for Teal runs deep.

"*Fuck.*" I bite out the curse. "Tanya was supposed to tell her. We agreed it was easier to take coming from her sister. But apparently that didn't fucking happen. What did she do?"

"She screamed at Stefano, scared half the guests, and then grabbed a bottle of Belvedere and ran into the break room where she's shitfaced and crying. I chased her down and made her take one of her Xanax before she could start chugging the vodka."

"Jesus Christ, Teal," I murmur, hating the idea that she's so unstable that we can't make a move without her chugging vodka and popping pills. *How the hell did we get to this point?*

217

The next thought through my brain is how the hell members are going to take it. "Where is she now?"

"Still in the break room. Every time either Tanya or I try to touch her, she screams and threatens to call the cops and tell them everything she's seen." In the background, muted voices go silent as Grice must step into an empty room.

"Jesus Christ," I whisper, opening the trash and tossing the half-eaten slice of pizza into it. "Teal's going to get herself killed that way. Fucking hell. I'm on my way. We have to get her out of there before Dom finds out what's happening."

"That's why I've been calling you. She's a nice girl, but she got caught off guard. You know she's delicate in a way that no one else is."

"I'll be right there. Keep her as quiet as you can. You just might save her life."

"I'll do whatever I can, Boss. Count on me."

I hang up and curse Tanya and Teal for ruining this night for me, but it doesn't do any good. I still have to leave Drew sleeping in my bed.

I tiptoe through the bedroom where her head is now tilted toward the opposite wall, and grab clothes out of my walk-in closet without turning on a light. Putting a suit back on is the last thing I want to do, but business always comes first.

Business shouldn't always come first. I can practically hear my mother's voice in my head, but regardless of whether that sentiment is right or not, I have no choice. Not if I don't want Teal to turn up missing, because then Tanya would go on the warpath, and I have no doubt it wouldn't end well.

I leave a note for Drew on the counter and slip out of the apartment, locking the door behind me.

DREW

J wake and sit up with a start, my eyes blinking rapidly as I try to focus on my surroundings.

Where the hell am I?

The smooth green sheets I'm lying on are imbued with a spicy, masculine cologne, and a tinge of musk that only comes from sex hangs in the air and on my skin. I know exactly where I am.

Cannon's place.

It's completely silent but for the sounds of the city drifting up from the street outside. Horns. A shout here or there. Doors slamming.

"Cannon?" I mouth his name silently at first, as if I'm scared to voice it. Or my throat is just dry as hell from screaming out in passion. Either one.

I listen harder for sounds of another person in his space, but it's eerily quiet.

"Cannon?" I call his name this time, but there's no answer. I swing my legs to the side of the bed and snag a dress shirt from the floor as my feet hit the weathered wood.

Slipping the shirt on, I luxuriate in being surrounded by

his scent as I pad from the bedroom out into the living room and kitchen area, looking for signs of life.

"Cannon?"

The third time I say his name without a response makes it official. He's gone. I scan the kitchen and my gaze lands on a piece of paper on the counter with my name written at the top in bold strokes.

Drew –
Had to take care of something at the club. Stay. I'll be back as soon as I can.

I read it a second time to make sure I'm not imagining words, but I'm not. He really left me sleeping in his bed to go back to work. The level of trust he's placed in me is completely and utterly unwarranted, and yet a warm feeling blooms in my chest.

My reporter instincts are telling me to use this time to search his office and dig into his files, but something holds me back. No, not something. *Everything.*

"Mine." I can still hear the possessive word echoing off the walls and ceilings. Never before in my life have I ever wanted anything to be more true.

I've never belonged to someone. The other half of a pair. A couple.

And you shouldn't be thinking about this now, because he's a target in your investigation.

I tell my inner voice to shut the hell up because I've already decided that Cannon *isn't* a target. I don't believe he could have been involved with my father's death. Not one single bit.

But when I slip back into the bathroom to take care of my

basic needs, I still open the almost invisible medicine cabinet and poke around inside. Not because I'm looking for leads or evidence, but because I'm looking for more *Cannon*. I spot a stick of deodorant and a bottle of cologne, and carefully pull them out one by one and sniff.

God, this is why he always smells so decadent. I commit the scents to memory and know I won't be able to smell them without thinking of him for the rest of my life.

When I flip on the water in the cavernous shower, I tell myself I'm only going to rinse off, but I take the opportunity to smell his soap as it lathers between my hands.

Yep, this is what I'm doing right now, and I don't care how pathetic it is.

Once I'm dry, I help myself to the robe hanging on the wall of the walk-in closet, and roll up the cuffs so they don't hang over my hands. As I wander out into the living room, I make my way to the stereo sitting on an industrial set of bookshelves. I'm surprised to see a turntable and an entire cage-fronted cabinet beneath it that is filled with records.

Records. As in vinyl. One of my weaknesses.

I spent my teen years collecting all of my father's favorites and gifted them to him with a refurbished turntable. He'd been thrilled, and every night, we'd spend an hour listening to them after he got home from broadcasting the evening news to the rest of America.

To them, he was Leander Lockwood, the confident voice that delivered bad news with compassion and good news with excitement. To me, he'd just been *Dad*.

The albums I'd given him over the years are all still resting in a place of honor in his home in Connecticut, which I'd been cleaning out when I found the stashed evidence that led me on this journey, where I met Cannon.

Right now I should be snooping through his office, trying

to build a case I could take to the Feds to bring down the entire Casso organization, but I can't bring myself to do it.

Not now.

I don't know if that makes me a piss-poor investigative journalist or simply human.

When I put on a Led Zeppelin album and listen to the strains of "The Rain Song," I push the self-recriminations out of my mind.

I can worry about everything else tomorrow. But right now I'm going to eat pizza and wait for my man to come back.

I just didn't realize it would be a long wait.

41

CANNON

"*A*re you seriously doing this right now?" I stare at Teal's tearstained and mascara-streaked cheeks as she clutches a bottle of Belvedere on the break-room floor, wedged in a corner.

Dammit, Grice. I curse him silently for his soft spot. *You should've taken it from her.*

It took a direct order to get Tanya out of here and back out serving a twenty-person meeting with Stefano, and I sent Grice back to the door, so it's just me and Teal for the moment. I should have taken this time with her earlier, sitting her down in my office and making sure she understood what was happening, but I didn't want a scene. Now I've got a fucking mess instead.

"You're really firing me." Her lips screw up into what I assume is supposed to be an expression that elicits sympathy, but all I see is an overemotional, entitled party girl who finally has to face the music.

I jam my hands in my pockets and stare down at her. "You're a shit employee, Teal. You know it and I know it."

"But—" She cuts off when I shake my head.

224

"I didn't say you were a bad person or a bad waitress, because you're not. You're damn good when you try, but your total lack of effort to even *show up* when you're supposed to is a joke. I shouldn't have to send a car service to get you four out of five nights. It's bullshit."

"I'm sorry," she wails.

"Put the goddamned bottle down, or it's coming out of your check." My commanding tone leaves no room for argument.

That gets her attention, and she lowers the bottle to the floor with a *thunk* as it hits the wood. "But I need the money."

It should be impossible to believe that this is the same woman who has charmed rich men from all walks of life into buying her jewelry, designer handbags, clothes, and God knows what else. If she'd been smart, she would have asked for more than just goods that would decline in value, like an apartment in her name. I know at least one or two men who would have bought it for her. But she doesn't know when to stop, and she always fucks up a good thing.

"If you could manage to show up on time and not be wasted or fucked up when you walk in the door, you'd have no problem collecting a paycheck."

Her shoulders shake as she snuffles. I want to feel sympathy for her, but it's hard when I've extended every single lifesaver available, and she's batted them all away for the last six months.

"I'm done with your shit, Teal. You're fired."

She looks up at me with blue eyes that are a perfect match to her sister's, blinking as big tears tip over the lids. "But I have a problem. I need help, Cannon. I can't stop. I don't know what to do."

Fuck. Me.

As if I've ever been able to walk away from someone who can admit they need help without my fucking offering it.

She could be playing me. It could be a scam. Or maybe Teal is finally wising up to the fact that she's a barely functional alcoholic who needs treatment desperately, and that's before we even get to whatever pills she's popping lately.

I crouch down into a squat and meet her tear-filled eyes. "What kind of help do you need, Teal? Tell me and we'll get it for you."

"She can't be prettier than me, can she?" More tears stream down her face as I stare at her in bafflement.

"What the hell are you talking about?"

"Your new girl. The waitress Tanya says you hired to replace me, and now you're banging her. Why not me, Cannon? I could've been your girl. I would've been so good at it. And now you're throwing me out, and I don't know what I'll do." She reaches for me.

I pop back up to my feet and pinch the bridge of my nose. "Are you fucking kidding me right now? Please say you're fucking kidding me."

"Jesus Christ, Teal. Stop before you embarrass yourself more," Tanya says from the doorway as she slips inside. "You said you wanted to hear that you were fired directly from Cannon. Now you have, so what the hell are you doing?"

With her bottom lip out and pouting, Teal shakes her head at both me and Tanya. "You know I wasn't serious about any of them. Just Cannon. But he never gave me a chance. That's why I tried to make him jealous with all of the others. But now he's *rejecting me*." The last two words come out with another wave of sobs.

I struggle not to reach out and tell the woman to get the fuck up and act like a goddamned adult and not a kid crying over something she can't have. But I can't find it in me to come down on her even more harshly while she's a goddamned mess.

"You always said you never touched employees. So *why her?*"

"Teal. Get up. You're going home," Tanya snaps the order and rushes around me.

"I don't want to go home until Cannon says I can stay!"

At Teal's begging, I harden my heart. It's the only way I can deal with her. As Tanya helps her off the floor, I square my shoulders.

"I'll pay you three months' severance, and Tanya will find you a treatment center where you'll be able to go to rehab. I'll cover the cost myself. If you decide to go and complete it, I'll help you find a job somewhere else when you're ready. You need help, Teal. It's time."

With one hand clasped in her sister's, Teal stares up at me like a princess who has just been told that her kingdom burned to ash.

"Rehab? I'm not a junkie!" She yanks on Tanya's hand and jerks away. "I swear I don't need rehab. Just some time. That's all."

As soon as she says *all*, Teal kicks over the bottle on the floor, and liquor spills all over my shoe and the carpet.

"Jesus, Teal. We all know you need to go to rehab. You can't beat this on your own," Tanya says quietly as Teal gasps.

I grit my teeth and close my eyes for a second to gather myself and my temper, but Teal takes it as an invitation. Her body slams against my chest, and her vodka-tinged lips sloppily press kisses against my mouth.

My eyes snap open, but Tanya's already got her by the shoulders, pulling her back and away from me.

"What the fuck, Teal?" her sister snaps, pushing her against the lockers.

"He loves me. I know he does. Cannon's always loved me. Why else would he be so nice to me?" She struggles against Tanya's hold.

"Fucking hell," Tanya whispers, wrapping her arms around her sister to calm her with a hug. "Teal, that's not true. You've made this up in your head."

"No! He loves me! I know it!"

I look at Tanya. "Get her out of here without making another scene. She's not coming back. Got it?"

Tanya nods with a sad look of acceptance on her face. "I'm so sorry, Cannon. I was going to tell her today, but I knew . . . I knew she wouldn't handle it well. I put it off to tomorrow, and it was a mistake. I fucked up, and you're well within your rights to fire me too."

"If he fires you, it's because he can't bear thinking about me, and that means he loves me!" Teal crows from her sister's arms.

What a fucking clusterfuck. I shake my head and meet Tanya's blue gaze.

"Find her a rehab place. If she'll go, send me the bill. No arguing."

Sadness etches lines deeper in Tanya's face than should be there at the age of twenty-seven, but that's not something I can change.

"You're a good man, Cannon."

"Take tomorrow off. Do whatever you need to do with Teal."

I don't reply to what she said about me being a good man. The jury's still out on that, pending the results of the roofie test I still haven't gotten back from Yoder. I make a mental note to call him tomorrow about the results, to make sure he hasn't forgotten.

"I'll get Grice, and he'll escort you both down to the car out the back way."

"Thank you."

"No! I won't go!"

Teal howls as I leave the break room and head back to my office, and I hope like hell no one else can hear her. When I step inside the hidden door, cigar smoke greets me in the hallway, where there should be none.

Fuck. That can only mean one thing.

Dom decided to hold a meeting tonight without letting me or the staff know, and he used the private elevator.

Except I'm wrong on one count—I find him sitting at my desk, ashing his cigar in a Baccarat crystal glass.

"Oh good, you're here. Which means you can tell me why the fuck you haven't dealt with Teal before it got ugly in front of club members."

I open my mouth to reply, but he holds up a hand.

"*After* you tell me why the hell you're making moves on the Rossettis before talking to me first, when we just struck a truce."

Fucking. Great.

42

DREW

*a*t the sound of the door closing and locking, I wake and jerk up in bed. Before I can rise, Cannon stands at the doorway to the bedroom. He looks like he got absolutely no sleep.

"What time is it?" I ask.

"Late. Or early, depending on how you want to look at it."

I glance around for a clock but find no glowing lights to orient me. "So . . . that means?"

"Six a.m. I've been up all fucking night, and it kills me to see you all mussed and in my bed, knowing I didn't get to be there with you."

Coming more awake, I blink a few times. "What happened at the club? Is everything okay?"

He shakes his head and looks so weary that I climb out, still in his robe, and move toward him. I don't know where the instinct comes from, but I feel like he needs a hug. Without another thought, I wrap my arms around Cannon and rest my cheek against his chest.

"I'm sorry for whatever happened."

"Teal happened, and it was her own fault."

230

I loosen my grip a fraction, not wanting to completely let him go, and glance up. "What do you mean?"

"She's an alcoholic and needs to go to rehab, but it'll be a miracle if she goes." He pauses, sweeping some hair out of my face and tucking it behind my ear. "She thinks she's in love with me."

I squint up at him. "Um . . . why?"

Cannon cups my jaw with one hand as he slides the other one around my back. "I didn't give her any reason to think that, if that's what you're asking."

In that moment, I realize I trust him too much to think he would do something like that intentionally and then start something with me. Maybe it's misplaced trust, but it's there all the same.

"I didn't think that. At all."

"Good, because it's not true. She's a nice girl. Probably too pretty for her own good, and no one taught her that she's got a hell of a lot more to offer to the world. According to Tanya, their dad walked out when they were young, and it fucked Teal up majorly."

A rush of sadness sweeps through me. "I'm sorry. I know you care about your employees. It's obvious from even the short amount of time that I've been working at the club. It must kill you to see her spiraling out of control without being able to help her."

He opens his mouth to reply, but his phone vibrates in his jacket pocket. Pulling in a deep breath, he tilts his head back and stares up at the ceiling in annoyance.

"I gotta take this. Dom's on my ass about Teal and the Rossettis. I hate to do this to you, but if you want to get your stuff, I'll take you home." He presses a kiss against my forehead. "I need you to work a double today, because neither Teal nor Tanya will be coming in. I'm really fucking sorry about that. I gotta rework the schedule for the next couple days, because I had some naive hope that Teal would work the rest of her shifts before she was done for good."

"If that's what I can do to help, don't worry about it. I'm happy to."

The lines of tension ease from his face as he tries to smile. "Thanks, babe. That means a lot to me."

In that moment, I can't help but wonder how many people go out of their way to do anything for this man, or if people count on him to be the steady, consistent one.

Yeah, and you were planning to betray him from day one, my inner voice whispers insidiously.

Not anymore, I snap back at it.

I step out of the warm circle of Cannon's arms and smile. "It'll just take me a second to get dressed. Sorry for borrowing your robe without asking."

The remains of the lines on his face fade away. "Don't ever apologize for that. It looks better on you than it ever has on me."

Ten minutes later, we're in the elevator heading down to the street level. But instead of leading me outside as I was expecting so we could ride back to my place in the Bentley, Cannon leads me through another door he unlocks.

"What is this?"

"You'll see."

He flips on the lights, and I realize it's a garage. In *Manhattan*. Inside it are three covered cars and a motorcycle.

"Are all these yours?" I ask the stupid question as he releases my hand to pull the cover off the one closest to the large overhead door.

"Yeah. Cars are a hobby. I met a guy down south who does a hell of a job restoring them, and that way I only wrench on them if I want to for fun."

He steps away, tugging the cover the rest of the way off, revealing a cherry-red muscle car with double white stripes slicing down the hood and chrome so shiny I can see my reflection.

"That is one sexy car." I spin to look at him in awe. "You've been hiding that in here?"

"Not hiding. Protecting. I take care of what's mine."

The last part might have been an offhand comment, but it works its way into that warm, fuzzy feeling in my chest along with the memory of him calling out *"Mine."*

"You ready for a hell of a ride home?"

I meet his hazel eyes and tell him the truth. "I'm going wherever you take me."

43

CANNON

a drive through the city in the morning, before the bumper-to-bumper traffic, is one of my favorite things. Normally, I hop in the car around three or four a.m., and really let the Chevelle go from grumbling to roaring down the streets, racing from light to light.

But none of those early morning drives has anything on today and *her*.

God, but the sight of Drew's dark hair blowing in the wind from the open window as she laughs when I turn and let the rear end break loose is the best damn thing I've ever seen or heard.

I knew falling for someone was supposed to make everything about them seem more special than it would be to an outsider, but I had no idea it would make a good moment become magical.

I'm so fucked.

And the kicker? I don't even care. I let this happen. Despite every warning sign, I've gone and done the one thing I've never done before. I've fucking fallen in love.

I didn't expect it to be this easy. I didn't expect it to

happen this fast. But like my mother said, *"Love doesn't care about time. It only needs the right moment."*

For years, I've wondered how she could have possibly gotten wrapped up in a man like Dominic Casso, but now I get it. It doesn't matter who a person truly is when your heart is making the decision—it shows you the best and the brightest of them as all of their faults fade away.

I'm willing to bet a hell of a lot of money, even this car that I'd wanted for twenty years before I got it, that nothing Drew is hiding could be as bad as what Dom hid from my mother. And even when she found out the truth, her dedication didn't waver.

Maybe that's how Freemans are built. We fall hard and fast like naive motherfuckers, and damn the consequences.

When I make the last right to turn down the street where Drew's building is located, she reaches out and squeezes my hand on the shifter.

"Thank you for last night. And this morning. Really, thank you for everything." Her turquoise eyes are shining, and the smile on her makeup-free face is everything I thought it would be. Absolutely stunning. Regal even. Like she was born to have men worshipping at her feet.

For the life of me, I can't figure out why she covers it all up, but I don't need to understand everything about her . . . yet.

"You're beautiful. Always, but especially just like this."

The blush I've seen rise from her chest actually does spread all the way to her bare cheekbones. Her dark lashes sweep down to contrast with her lightly tanned skin and a few freckles.

When she looks back up at me, there's a serious expression on her face. "I never let anyone see me like this. Ever."

"Why?"

She presses her lips together, hesitating. I'm waiting for a pithy deferral, but instead, she gives me something different. "It's complicated. I really, really want to tell you why, though. I just . . . I'm afraid of how you're going to react."

I want to tell her that she can tell me anything right now. That it won't change a thing. But I'm not sure that's the truth yet, and I don't want to give her anything but.

"Tomorrow morning, I want to see you the same way, except still soft and warm from sleep, in my bed. How about you tell me then? No more pretenses. No more lies."

An uncertain expression crosses her face before she takes a deep breath. "I would really, really like that. It's time." The uncertainty morphs into sadness as she pulls her hand back, and I have a feeling I'm not going to like what she has to say.

I double-park in front of her building and shift the Chevelle into neutral. This time, I grab her fingers and tangle them with mine.

"Whatever you're hiding from, I promise I can handle it. I've got strong shoulders. Put your burden on me."

I don't know where that came from, but I mean it. I want to make her life easier. Want to ease the worry and edginess that seems second nature to her. *Hell, I really am well and truly fucked.*

"You might want to hold off on believing that until you hear what I have to say," she says with her brows knitting together.

"Let me worry about that. I'll see you at the club. I'll send Warren over to get you."

Drew squeezes my hand and leans over to press a kiss on my lips. "You're a good man, Cannon."

With a hand slipping into her hair, I take the kiss deeper, memorizing the taste of her lips, until someone honks from behind us. I throw up a middle finger out the window and don't pull back until I'm good and ready.

"The world can go to hell when I'm with you," I whisper.

Drew's entire face softens. "I'll see you soon," she replies, fumbling for her purse and her jacket while trying to open the door.

The contents of her purse spill on the floor as she tries to maneuver the old-school handle, and I try not to blink when I realize I was right and she does have two cell phones. I tell myself I'm not betraying everything I just said and thought when I help her gather her things up from the floorboards and *accidentally* shove the iPhone with no case—the one that her mom called on—beneath the seat while she's climbing out.

"I think you got it all."

From behind me, the car honks again, and I take it as a reason to get the hell out of there with a wave at the girl I know is hiding something big.

I might be in love, but I'm still a cautious motherfucker.

I've learned one cardinal rule from Dom while living under his reign—never walk into a situation you're not eminently prepared to confront. Otherwise, it might cost you your life.

When I fish the phone out from the seat, I stare down at the screen.

Whatever Drew plans to tell me tomorrow morning, I plan on already knowing it.

*T*omorrow. *Tomorrow. Tomorrow.*

That's all I can repeat in my head over and over, because I have to figure out a way to come clean and not end up with Cannon hating me.

Hating me? Is that what I'm really worried about? I should be more worried about him turning me over to Dom, who probably still encases people's feet in concrete before tossing them off a pier.

Falling for Cannon has changed everything, though. *But how the hell am I going to tell him everything?*

I still haven't come up with an answer four and a half hours later when Warren pulls up in front of my building with the Escalade.

"Good morning, Ms. Carson," he says, and I try not to wince. My alias grates on my ears when he says it.

"Good morning, Warren. How are you?"

"Can't complain. It's another day in paradise."

I settle in the back of the car and pull out my phone to do some mindless scrolling during the ride, but when I open my purse, a terrifying realization hits me hard.

I only have one phone. Where is my other phone?

I dig around in my purse, but I don't see it. I'm not imagining that it's not here. My brain skips back to this morning when I couldn't open a door handle from the 1970s and spilled everything on the floorboard of Cannon's car.

No. No. No. I didn't leave it there. I didn't. I wouldn't have. I couldn't have. It has to be back in my apartment in the clothes I wore home.

Right? Of course. That's exactly where it is.

It's going to be fine.

Totally fine.

But I'm lying to myself, just like I've lied to Cannon since the moment my résumé landed on his desk. And tomorrow I'm going to tell him everything and hope to live to see the next day . . . without him hating me forever.

Jesus Christ, I'm a fucking idiot. Who thought this was a good plan? Surely not me. Because it sounds like the absolute worst plan in the entire world.

He won't hurt me. He couldn't. That's one thing I do truly believe. But how the hell do I think it's going to turn out when I put Cannon in the position where he's keeping something vital from Dom? I could get *him* killed.

At that thought, every single drop of blood in my body runs cold.

I can't do that to him. I love him.

Oh fuck. Fuck. Fuck. Fuck.

A strangled sound escapes my throat, and Warren meets my gaze in the rearview mirror.

"You okay, Ms. Carson?"

That name. Again. It's like nails on a chalkboard or someone crunching on shards of glass.

No, don't think about things like torture.

239

I can't do this. I can't do any of this, but I nod for Warren's sake.

What the fuck am I going to do now? How am I going to fix the mess I've made?

My first instinct is to run. Far and fast, and call leaving my heart in New York City in the safekeeping of Cannon Freeman as my penance for thinking I could do this. But the car keeps rolling toward the Upper Ten. Short of opening the door and throwing myself out into oncoming traffic, there's nothing I can do to stop the chain of events I've unleashed.

My heart rate kicks up, and my palms sweat.

Stay cool. Act cool. Be cool. I silently repeat my mantra before I realize I need more than that. I need someone a hell of a lot smarter than me to weigh in.

Desperate, I stare up at the ceiling of the car.

Dad, what would you do? Please give me some kind of guidance, because I'm in really fucking deep and I'm about to be in over my head.

After my silent prayer for assistance, I wait for any sign from him or the universe to light up in neon, telling me how to fix things before I destroy it all.

But when we stop in front of the building housing the club, I still have zero answers. I thank Warren for the ride and hop out of the car with as much enthusiasm as a death row inmate walking toward the lethal injection room.

To make matters worse, the man who will stand as my executioner is waiting for the elevator when I step inside.

"Drew, good to see you again. How are things?"

Dominic Casso's voice, a slightly deeper version of his son's, is enough to raise every hair on the back of my neck. But it's his stare, those nearly black, all-seeing eyes, that unnerves me as they drill into mine, searching for all my hidden secrets.

My mortality, something I didn't think about too often before this investigation, is now at the forefront of my mind. *I may not live to see the weekend.* My stomach churns, and with each flop, the knot that takes up residence there grows bigger and more heinous.

Why did I think I was smart enough to take on the mob? I'm not. At all. And this cagey old man gesturing for me to enter the elevator ahead of him is going to be the end of life as I know it.

The foreboding feeling follows me all the way up to the club as he makes small talk, but I'm so distracted, I couldn't tell you what he asked or what I answered. If there's a quiz later, I'm fucked.

Actually, skip the quiz. I'm just fucked. All around.

When Grice opens the door to the club, there's a kind smile on his craggy face.

"Good morning, Mr. Casso. Ms. Carson."

"Grice," the older man replies with a nod. "Where's Cannon?"

Grice reaches for the interior door and swings it open for us, but my feet stick to the carpet like they've been glued down.

"Not here at present, sir. He was in this morning and then left to run an errand. Said he'd be back as soon as he could."

I shuffle ahead, trying to at least pretend I'm not eavesdropping like it's my job as Dom replies.

"He's not answering his cell, and I have a matter I need to discuss with him. Urgently."

When Grice glances at me, I know I need to move along before I attract more attention. I take another step forward, wondering why Dom didn't just call the club to ask if Cannon was here instead of showing up in person.

Probably because he doesn't want to discuss it on the phone.

Then why would he call Cannon's cell? I succeed in moving into the main area of the club and don't overhear any more of the conversation that wasn't meant for my ears.

Letty waves at me from the bar, and I take a few steps toward her.

"What's up, Letty?"

With a laugh, she shoots me a wink. "Nothing. Just wondering how I could get the boss to run errands for me. You must have him wrapped around your finger, girl."

I stare at her in confusion. "What are you talking about?"

"Cannon going to pick your mom up at the airport. He hurried out of here . . ."

As she trails off at what must be a look of horror on my face, my blood goes from running cold to frozen completely solid, and static fills my ears.

She didn't say what I think she said. It's not possible. That's impossible. No. No. No.

"I guess you didn't know?" Letty adds, her eyes widening as footsteps come to a halt just behind me.

Dominic Casso's gruff voice interrupts the heart failure I'm currently undergoing. "Say that again, Letty. You know where Cannon's at?"

CANNON

I see absolutely no similarity between Drew Carson and her mother. None at all, at least, not the real Drew.

Except, there is no *real Drew*.

"I can't believe Memphis ignored my calls *and* didn't bother to tell me she had such a handsome man in her life. I really appreciate the ride. My daughter always arranges a car service for me because she knows that I don't have the slightest clue how to do any of that. I wasn't meant for work. I'm purely here as ornamentation, as I'm sure you can tell." The woman's hand skims along my arm, and I move farther onto my side of the car.

"But this car. Good gracious. It makes me think of all those crazy parties we used to have back in the day." She shakes her blond hair, its color straight out of a bottle, and not a wig.

As much as I wish I could shut her up because every word out of her mouth is a stab to my gut, I can't. There's no shutting up Mrs. Leander Lockwood.

Leander Lockwood. Memphis Lockwood's father. The most

recognizable news anchor in the history of broadcasting, who fathered a tenacious investigative journalist who has blown open case after case and helped put dozens of people in jail.

I'm a goddamned fucking idiot. This is what happens when you think with your dick.

Betrayal and anger bubble just beneath the surface like a boiling-hot pool of magma. I'm a goddamned volcano about to erupt, and when I do, it's not going to be on the self-absorbed woman in the seat beside me. No, it'll wait until after I drop her off at the Plaza, *where she doesn't even have a room booked because she doesn't do that kind of thing herself.*

I suck in a deep breath, focusing on the road and listening to every word of her inane chatter. It fills in so many fucking blanks, I don't know how I missed them all.

"Memphis was always a daddy's girl. She and I never got along. I think it's because people always mistook us for best friends instead of stepmother and daughter. Because obviously it's clear she couldn't possibly be my child. This body hasn't gone through childbirth."

She laughs in what is probably supposed to be a seductive manner, but it comes off as brittle and bitter as she smiles over at me with her perfectly applied mauve lipstick.

"She's probably already told you all that. She's her father's *accident* from a prior relationship. Can you believe he didn't even tell me he had a child when we got married? I didn't sign up for that, but I was a team player when he brought her home one day. I was never meant to be a mother, though. I think that gene missed me, but I did my best. Not that she's ever been grateful for it."

I exit the highway, wishing I could punch the gas harder instead of having to brake. I want this woman out of my car as fast as possible, but thankfully, she doesn't notice a damn thing except the sound of her own voice.

"She couldn't even bother to answer the phone when I called. Always so busy with work." Finally, she glances at me. "Do you know what she's working on now? Or is she keeping that a secret from you too?"

My teeth grind together, and my molars threaten to crack under the pressure. It takes me a moment before I can even summon words to answer her because the truth is *I am her daughter's fucking investigation.* I don't have to hear it from *Memphis* to know.

"Not sure," I bite out, but in my brain, I'm raging.

What the fuck is she thinking, trying to dig into the goddamned fucking mob? Does she want to end up dead? Does she want to get me killed too? No, she probably just wants to see me behind bars.

How could I have been so fucking stupid? The signs were all there. The wig. The contacts. The two phones. The bits and pieces of information she shared.

And I still fell in love with the little liar, who I now want to pick up and shake until every single fucking bit of the truth falls from her sweet, lying lips.

It's a miracle that my ability to turn rage to ice is still functioning, because other than the day my mother had been killed, I've never wanted to destroy everything I can lay my hands on.

And right beside me, her stepmother keeps going.

"I really hope they have a suite left for me. I'm one of the Plaza's most valued customers, you know. Leander always kept an apartment here in the city, but I never wanted to stay in it. I told him that important people always stay at the Plaza, because how else is anyone going to know they're here? If there was ever a man who was completely untrainable, it was Leander. I know the entire world thought he was

245

infallible, but he was a regular man like everyone else. I just wish he hadn't encouraged Memphis the way he did. She went off to Columbia to get her journalism degree—"

Columbia. Which wasn't on her fucking résumé because that would have made her way too overqualified for the goddamned job, I think as her mom keeps going without taking a breath.

"And she didn't even have a single boyfriend the entire time. I'm sure every other girl in her class snapped up the good ones while she had her nose buried in books. She really could've benefited from more of my influence, but she only listened to her father."

Even though I'm seething behind my polite mask, I can't help but feel a single pang of thankfulness. I'm fucking thankful that *Memphis* didn't benefit from any more of her mother's influence. Except . . . if she had, then there would be no way in hell I would have ever fallen for her.

Blessing or curse? I don't even know. How fucked up is that?

When I pull up in front of the Plaza, I waste no time popping the trunk and getting the fuck out of the car to get Mrs. Lockwood's bag.

Lockwood. Memphis Lockwood. Even as her name floats through my brain, I can picture the reporter on TV, but she doesn't look like my Drew . . . at least, not really.

Except she's not my Drew. *She's a goddamned chameleon.*

"I never let anyone see me like this. Ever." Her words from this morning come back with a vengeance, and now I understand exactly why she never let anyone see her in the one guise she couldn't change.

When I place Mrs. Lockwood's Louis Vuitton luggage on the bellhop's cart that appeared as efficiently as ever, she smiles at me.

"It was so nice to meet you, Mr. Freeman. Do tell

Memphis that I'll be free for dinner tomorrow evening, and I expect her to take me out somewhere nice. A Michelin-starred restaurant, obviously."

I literally have nothing to say to this woman, so I just nod. "I'll let *Memphis* know."

Without even waiting to find out if she can get a room, I jump back in my car and punch the gas, needing the angry growl of the engine to drown out my thoughts. They all pretty much center around one thing—

Today Memphis Lockwood is telling me the goddamned truth and nothing else.

46

DREW

Oh God. Oh God. Oh God.

Dom thankfully left the club with orders to have Cannon come to his office right away when he returned, but that doesn't mean I've calmed down even remotely.

I nearly spill the tray of entrées I'm trying to deliver to the table in the most private corner of the club. Silas Bohannon, the actor from my first day, sits at the foot of the table with a few other men.

Do not fuck this up. Or maybe I should? Then I would get fired, and I could run away and never come back.

Except, my father didn't raise a coward. No, he raised a strong woman with balls of steel, who wasn't afraid of anyone or anything and worshipped at the almighty altar of the truth.

What would Leander Lockwood do? He probably wouldn't have fallen in love with his target, for starters.

No, strike probably. That's a *definitely*.

I paste the most genuine imitation of a smile I can on my face as I deliver the salmon Caesar salad to Silas first. "Here you go, sir."

"Thank you, Drew."

Drew. My fake name is like a cymbal clashing in my head as I wait for Cannon to return and cast judgment.

"How are you doing today?" Silas asks.

The rest of the men at the table stop talking and stare at Silas like he's a freak of nature for speaking to the help. I don't recognize the others, so I assume they're entertainment industry types, and not actors.

"Very well, thank you." I respond as politely as possible, not wanting to engage in conversation because I'm too busy freaking out inside over the coming confrontation with Cannon.

I quickly deliver the rest of the plates and stop next to Silas again. "Is there anything else I can get you, gentlemen?"

Everyone at the table says no and promptly ignores me to start eating, except for Silas. He doesn't even reach for his silverware or the linen napkin to drop on his lap. He just stares at me.

"Something wrong?" he asks. "You seem tense."

"I'm fine. Totally fine." I smile tightly, and he sees right through me. I suppose as an actor, you're more likely to recognize when someone is *acting.*

"Have you lived in the city long?" he asks.

I have no idea why he's making small talk with me and ignoring his guests. Smiling again, I say, "Long enough."

His head tilts to the side as he studies me. "Have you ever lived in LA? You seem really familiar. I thought it last time I was here, and now I swear I've seen you somewhere before."

Heavy hands clamp down on my shoulders, keeping me grounded as opposed to jumping out of my skin at the fright. I don't need to turn around to know who it is. Cannon's scent and the anger rolling off him tell me plenty.

"Drew has one of those familiar faces. Don't you, *Drew?"*

His fingers tighten their grip, almost to the point of pain but stopping short.

He knows. I know he knows. He knows I know he knows too.

Jesus Christ. What a clusterfuck.

"Funny, I swear it's more than that." Silas's gaze skips from me to Cannon and then back again, stalling on the way Cannon's touching me.

Hell, Silas probably knows too.

"It's a pleasure to see you again, Mr. Bohannon," Cannon says. "If there's anything you need, don't hesitate to ask. Letty will be taking over your service. I have to borrow *Drew* for a bit."

Something in my gut tells me that if I were to mouth the word *help*, Silas is the kind of man who wouldn't hesitate to jump in and save me from Cannon, but that wouldn't do me any good, actually. It would be the worst possible thing I could do.

Instead, I smile and nod. "Enjoy your lunch, Mr. Bohannon."

Cannon's heavy hands lift off my shoulders. He spears me with a glare and says nothing before turning and walking toward the entrance of the Upper Ten.

Shit. Shit. Shit.

I don't dare do anything but follow him. Emotion rolls off him in nearly visible waves, and all I can think is, *Thank you, God. It's been a good ride. Whatever happens next, I know I brought it on myself.*

Cannon strides back into the entryway, and Grice opens the door for us.

"Boss, you want me to let Mr. Casso know you're on your way?"

"No."

Cannon's clipped reply causes Grice's head to jerk back.

"But he said it was urgent. Sounded important. You might want to—" Grice stops speaking when Cannon's head swings toward him.

"I'll handle it. Hold down the fort. Tell Letty she's on her own. If she needs help, call Stefano in."

With that, Cannon stalks out of the Upper Ten and punches the elevator call button.

I stop six feet away from him, and as soon as the door closes quietly behind me, Cannon's gaze sharpens to an even more vicious point. I open my mouth, not even sure what I'm going to say, but he holds up a hand.

"Don't say a fucking word until I tell you to."

Whatever happens next, I already know my life will never be the same.

47

CANNON

*J*ust seeing her has the ice encasing my rage thawing, and by the time we reach my car in the garage, it's growing hotter and hotter. I walk to the passenger door and practically rip it off its hinges.

"Get in."

Drew—no, Memphis—presses her lips together hard, flattening them. Lips I've kissed. Lips that have told me more lies than anyone has ever managed. Just looking at her makes me want to break something.

She opens her mouth, and I glare at her.

"Not gonna say it again. Get in the fucking car and don't say a goddamned word."

To her credit, her eyes don't well up with crocodile tears. That's something, at least.

She slides inside, and I slam the passenger door. Rounding the front, I barely stop myself from putting a fist-sized dent in the cherry-red hood.

Women. They're going to be the fucking death of me. That's one thing I know for sure.

Warren pops his head out of who the hell knows where. "Boss? Can I drive you somewhere?"

"No."

"Mr. Casso was looking for you. He called my cell, checking to see if you were with me."

I grip the chrome door handle until the metal should threaten to bend. "I'll find him when I'm ready."

Warren's gray eyebrows shoot up to his receding hairline. "He said it was urgent, Boss. He sounded serious."

I release the handle and take three steps toward him. I've always wondered if I could trust Warren, and my confidence is dropping with every moment.

"You didn't see me. Got it? If I find out you told him you saw me, you won't ever want to fucking see me again."

The threat underlying my tone has Warren stumbling back a step.

"Sorry, Boss. I didn't see anything. He won't hear it from me."

The shock on his face tells me I've made a very grave tactical mistake. *Never let anyone see your anger. It just makes them more suspicious about what's going on.*

Whatever.

It's not every fucking day you find out that the woman you were falling for is going to get you and herself killed. *Fucking Christ.*

I stalk back to the car and yank open the door and slide in. The only thing that remotely soothes the raging beast in my soul is the roar of the big block as I rev the engine. All I want to do is drive straight the fuck out of town, but I can't. Not yet. Not until I find out what the hell she was doing and come up with a plan.

Instead, I haul ass out of the garage and crank the wheel to the right, cutting off a cab that lays on its horn. I don't

253

even bother to throw up the middle finger. He can suck my dick.

We can't go far. Not without making Dom more suspicious than he already is. The fact that he's so desperate to find me tells me I'm already dealing with a big fucking problem. I can count on one hand the number of times he's been that insistent on tracking me down, and every goddamned time, someone was either about to die or already dead.

I blow through a yellow light, drive a few more blocks, and ignore the woman sitting in the passenger seat. To her credit, she hasn't said a word.

I change lanes, finally having a destination in mind. Just over the river in Jersey City, we've got a construction site for a new storage building that is waiting on permits.

When we take the bridge, I glance over at Drew. No, *Memphis. Memphis fucking Lockwood. Ace reporter. Investigative journalist wunderkind.*

Not trusting that Dom couldn't have bugged my car or had Warren do it while I was upstairs in the club, I stay quiet for another twenty minutes until I slow in front of a construction entrance. When we turn in, Memphis shrinks against the door of the car.

"Jesus Christ. Really?"

When I look over, she's grabbing the door handle, ready to jump out and run for her life.

Good to know she trusts me too. The fact that she's shaking pisses me off even more. *She thinks I'm just going to bring her to a construction site and bury her fucking body? Really? Is that who she thinks I am?*

A second round of anger ignites deep in my soul.

"Not a goddamned word until we get out."

I felt it and she didn't. It was all a fucking job to her.

I don't know what's worse—knowing that Dom will want

retribution, or knowing that I was so fucking wrong about her.

After I throw the Chevelle into park, I get the fuck out and stalk toward the metal skeleton of framework waiting for crews to come put on the roof and walls. Seagulls scream overhead, dipping and circling until they're practically screeching in my ear.

A crunch in the gravel comes from behind me but I keep my back to her, half wondering if she's packing and going to put a bullet in my back.

Then I remember I'm the offspring of a mobster, not her.

The footsteps stop, and I jam my hands into my pockets before turning around to face her, taking in the wig and the contacts and the blank mask on her face.

It's almost possible to make myself forget how I feel about Memphis Lockwood when she's masquerading as Drew Carson. *Almost.*

I swallow all the things I want to say in favor of one question to start off the last discussion I ever wanted to have with her. I yank her phone out of my pocket and hold it between two fingers.

"Do you have a fucking death wish?"

48

MEMPHIS

My entire body shakes as tremors of fear rip through me. The son of New York's most infamous mobster brought me to an abandoned construction site in Jersey. If that's not the start of a story that ends in getting offed by the mob, I don't know what is. I flex my palms, trying to pretend they're not clammy, wishing they were gripping a weapon, and that the man in front of me is someone I could actually shoot if I had one.

God, I really fucked this up. I could blame my mother, but it's not her fault that I'm here. She was just a variable I didn't count on screwing me over this morning.

I try to think of something to say in reply. Anything. But the deception that comes so easily to me in any other situation is absent. Because I can't lie to Cannon. Not anymore.

"I just want to know who killed my father for investigating the Casso family."

Cannon glances skyward, and the only witnesses to him trying to control his temper are the seagulls hovering around us, waiting for scraps or to crap on our heads. Given how my day's going, the latter is more likely.

Would that be considered gallows humor?

Cannon rakes his gaze over my face before jamming a hand into his hair, mussing it completely. "Crazy fucking woman. Do you know what the fuck you've done? Do you have any goddamned idea?"

My first urge is to curl into myself, but I refuse to cower. "Is it stupid to want vengeance for the death of the only person who ever loved you? Is it really?" My voice shakes as I continue. "You watched your mother be gunned down. So tell me, Cannon Freeman, could you walk away from that without wanting justice?"

"Don't fucking talk about my mother. She doesn't have a single fucking thing to do with this. Other than the fact that her getting involved with Dom got her killed. Just like you sniffing around him is going to get you killed." His hands flex before curling into fists as he paces the gravel.

I swallow the lump in my throat, but I shouldn't be surprised. I knew that what I was doing carried more risk than any investigation I've undertaken before.

"Did he do it? If I'm going to die, just fucking tell me the truth. Did he order my father's death?" I wrap an arm around my middle, as if bracing for the blow that will end me.

Cannon, the man who I let get closer to me than any man in my life, spins around and stomps away from me before pausing to let loose a roar of rage.

When he stalks back, his nostrils flaring, I stand my ground, even though I want to run. But my father didn't raise a deserter. I put these wheels of fate into motion, and I'll see it through. For better or for worse. No matter how stupid that is.

"Are you fucking serious? You think I know about every single goddamned hit? You think we keep a record book? A list of names, all neatly printed, just in case some snooping reporter wants to come in and find evidence to bring down the whole organization? Jesus Christ, woman. That's not how it fucking works. What the fuck were you even thinking? You were never gonna find evidence of something like that. *Ever.*"

Now probably isn't the best time to mention that I didn't care what kind of evidence I found. I just wanted whoever was responsible in prison.

"So you don't know?" I ask, holding tight to the reason I started this.

Gravel crunches beneath Cannon's loafers as he closes the distance between us once more. He shoves my phone into my hand and then reaches up to grip both of my shoulders.

"If you had any fucking clue how badly I want to shake the shit out of you right now for being so goddamned stupid and reckless, you'd be running in the other direction."

I refuse to shrink. I refuse to back down. I hold his stare with my own.

"What other choice did I have? The cops refused to listen to me. They treated me like a teenager with a conspiracy theory. I know my father didn't shoot himself. I don't give a fuck what they said. Someone killed him, and I want justice."

Cannon squeezes his eyes closed for a second, and then his fingers dig into my jacket and his hazel eyes blaze.

"Justice. Like that's even real. It won't fucking bring him back. Nothing will. Trust me, I wanted to burn down the world when my mother was murdered. Not a goddamned thing took away any of the pain. You understand me? This is a losing battle. All you did is the one thing your father never would've wanted you to do—put yourself in danger. And then you went and dragged me into it."

I bite down on my lip, hard. "I'm sorry, Cannon. I'm sorry for lying to you. For dragging you into this. You didn't deserve it. I knew, almost immediately, that you couldn't have had anything to do with this at all. I used you, and I shouldn't have. I'm sorry."

At first, my apology falls on deaf ears. Nothing changes in Cannon's expression when I say those words. As I open my mouth to repeat *I'm sorry* over and over again until he finally believes me, he releases his hold on my shoulders, and his hands lift to cradle my face. I can't tell if he wants to rip my head off or kiss me.

"I'm a stupid fucking prick for even asking this question, but I have to know. Was any of it fucking real?"

Before I can answer, the sound of an engine revving comes from behind us, and Cannon lets go of my face and shoves me behind him. I peek around his shoulder to see a black sedan roll into the construction site.

"Fuck," Cannon whispers.

The back door opens as soon as it parks, and out steps Dominic Casso.

"This isn't my fucking office, Cannon." He walks toward us, the gravel crunching beneath his feet sounding like a death knell.

"I'm handling it."

Dom's chin lifts. "Handling what exactly?"

"Go back to your office, Dom. I'll be there in a few minutes."

Terror, unlike anything I've ever known, rushes through my system. But not for me. For Cannon. The way Dom glares at him is enough to freeze my blood.

"What the fuck did you just say to me, boy? You did not just tell me to go, did you?" Dom's head tilts like he's truly never heard those words spoken to him before.

"With all due respect, sir, I'm busy right now." Cannon's tone turns deadly.

With a humorless laugh, Dom reaches inside his jacket. Cannon tenses, pushing me farther behind him.

Jesus Christ. Even after everything I've done to him, he's still protecting me, and I definitely don't deserve it. But if there's any way I can get us out of this alive, I will.

I glance around at the ground, looking for any kind of weapon to fight back. *Wait, maybe Cannon has one—*

My thought is cut off when Dom pulls out a pistol and transfers it to his other hand, his fingers wrapped around the barrel and the grip facing Cannon.

"It's time to prove yourself, kid. You take care of her, or I will."

Cannon and Memphis's story will be complete in White Knight, *the second book of the Dirty Mafia Duet.*

ABOUT THE AUTHOR

Making the jump from corporate lawyer to romance author was a leap of faith that *New York Times*, #1 *Wall Street Journal*, and *USA Today* bestselling author Meghan March will never regret. With over thirty titles published, she has sold millions of books in nearly a dozen languages to fellow romance-lovers around the world. A nomad at heart, she can currently be found in the woods of the Pacific Northwest, living her happily ever after with her real-life alpha hero.

She would love to hear from you. Connect with her at:
Website: meghanmarch.com
Facebook: @MeghanMarchAuthor
Twitter: @meghan_march
Instagram: @meghanmarch

Beneath This Ink

Beneath These Chains

Beneath These Scars

Beneath These Lies

Beneath These Shadows

Beneath The Truth

DIRTY BILLIONAIRE TRILOGY:

Dirty Billionaire

Dirty Pleasures

Dirty Together

DIRTY GIRL DUET:

Dirty Girl

Dirty Love

REAL DUET:

Real Good Man

Real Good Love

REAL DIRTY DUET:

Real Dirty

Real Sexy

FLASH BANG SERIES:

Flash Bang

Hard Charger

STANDALONES:

Take Me Back

Bad Judgment

Made in the USA
Lexington, KY
26 November 2019